Etan didn't have to look at Alex to know he was biting his tongue, dying to say something. He could feel how tense Alex's leg was against his own, could just about hear his agitation.

"What are you wanting to say, Alex?"

"If we have to set you up as a prophet, that's what we need to do. I hated what happened in Maple Ridge and everywhere else. But we can't have gone through so much hell to get here and let everything fall apart again. If people will follow the Great Prophet Etan and that lets us survive, then that's who you need to be."

Etan did groan then, closing his eyes for a second. Not only because this was what he'd been afraid of. Because the words and the ideas sounded true.

They *felt* true, no matter how much he might dislike them.

"I don't know if I can agree to that, not right now. I have no idea how to do any of this, much less create a new religion. I'm scared to death of making a hard situation worse."

Fighting the Storm: Book Four of the Storms of Future Past Series

Copyright © 2019 by Kari A. Kilgore

Published 2019 by Spiral Publishing, Ltd.
www.spiralpublishing.net

ISBN-13: 978-1-948890-12-0
Library of Congress Control Number: 2019942219

To Kelly

For helping bring these babies into the world.

FIGHTING THE STORM

BOOK FOUR OF THE STORMS OF FUTURE PAST SERIES

KARI KILGORE

SPIRAL PUBLISHING, LTD.

PART I

COMING BACK TO LIFE

Late March in Wolf Branch, Virginia, was beautiful and pleasantly unpredictable.

A soft, warm breeze drifting across the forested mountains surrounding the town felt like spring. The faint pink blush washing across the trees promised flowers, leaves, and fruit to come. Children begged to go out without coats or even long sleeves, and adults often followed, eager to work the soil for early planting.

The simple promise of sun against skin brought people, animals, and the earth back to full life after winter's long hibernation.

One short day later, heavy gray clouds blocked the mountaintops and the sky before delivering a late blizzard with a couple of feet of snow to bring everything to a temporary halt.

An all-powerful reminder that winter still held sway.

Temperatures plunged to well below freezing, eager to take out much of that early planting with a good hard frost. Kids delighted with one last snowball fight and chance to build their own tiny towns full of blinding white buildings and creatures. Adults smiled and shook their heads, knowing they'd take the chance again next year for the potential reward of fresh vegetables.

In days past, snowplows and salt trucks would have rolled out, ready to keep the neat grid of streets cleared before the first flakes fell. Driving and walking to the businesses and shops might have been slow going, but entirely possible.

Residents of the close-knit Appalachian town tucked into a bend of the winding Grasspe River would have grumbled, bundled up, and made their cautious last-minute runs for bread, milk, and beer just ahead of the storm. Back home, they would have enjoyed the chance to relax, warm and full, confident in the knowledge that empty store shelves would be full once the snow melted.

Folks who lived farther out along the twisting, narrow roads might have fared a little bit worse with a sudden change in the weather. Valley roads that rarely saw the sun sometimes stayed dangerous or impassable for days. But as long as firewood and pantry supplies held out, people in the deep hollows around Wolf Branch had no real problems.

Worries of keeping enough gas on hand for generators and frequent power outages had dwindled nearly half a century before, with a modern power grid driven by an experimental windmill farm near the mountaintop community of Maple Ridge. The majority of vehicles that navigated the tricky snowed-in roads were electric and guided by automatic navigation systems.

Even in such a remote and pristine area, surrounded by hundreds of acres of re-grown wilderness, all the convenience and security of the passing of the fossil fuel era eased modern lives.

Even in the middle of an unexpected March blizzard.

Until the end of the world changed everything.

Chapter 1

Alex Collins stepped outside the white cinderblock walls of the Wolf Branch cannery, wiping a couple of hours' worth of maintenance gunk from his hands. His breath rose in a white plume, a lot like the wood smoke rising from houses and buildings all around him. Aside from those plumes, the town spread out silent and still below where he stood.

His curly red hair was longer than it had been for a while, brushing his shoulders. His full winter beard would be ready for a springtime trim once warm weather finally arrived.

He breathed deep, taking in the warm, homey scent of burning wood. What he affectionately called the original means of heating with stored solar energy. That comforting smell and the quiet would have been unimaginable to him only a few short years ago, when he still lived in Chicago.

The community garden and greenhouse that Alex and nearly everyone in Wolf Branch had worked so hard to get going still held the remains of an unusually late snow. The curved roof of the greenhouse shed just like it was supposed to, leaving a nearly waist-deep drift all around its edges. The garden waited for planting, flat except for a few leftover stands of kale standing defiant and tall.

The greenhouse already held seedlings started a few weeks ago and a few rows of spring greens. Alex could see bright yellow, pink, and other shades from flowers they managed to grow all year long through the transparent sides. Those traces of color always made him smile.

Some were for practical purposes, like the edible nasturtium and medicinal herbs. But the flowers grown just because they were pretty were Alex's favorites.

The red brick school towering three stories to his right was as empty as the parking lot, waiting for safer conditions to start regular classes. Most of the school-aged kids in Wolf Branch lived in town, close enough to walk to school. Several of them would be descending on the cannery shortly with their parents in tow, most on foot.

Carpool lanes and school buses were in the past.

The solid thunk of a door closing behind him, followed by footsteps on the concrete floor of the cannery made Alex smile again. A warm hand grabbed his.

"And you accuse *me* of liking the cold."

Alex turned into the embrace of his husband Etan. Four months and more than the usual amount of troubled hours passing hadn't dulled his pleasure in those two words.

My husband.

"Cold outside is one thing," Alex said. "You're the one who wants to see your breath in the bedroom."

"Easier to warm up in there. When will everyone get here?"

"Any time now. I think everything inside is ready for spring. Shouldn't be any more surprises."

Etan leaned back and smiled, but his green eyes were sad. That sorrow lifted more and more often now, sometimes for days at a time. Finding bits of shattered glass and grime behind a storage cabinet earlier that morning - remnants of the attack that had taken the life of Etan's father - had brought the sorrow back full force for both of them.

"I can deal with the things I expect to see every day, you know?" Etan said. "It's the things I don't expect that get me."

Alex couldn't stop himself from glancing at the steep, curving road going past the cannery. A darker patch of pavement, rougher and not quite level, marked the spot where his father-in-law had lost his life. And quite likely saved everyone else's.

Both men turned at the unusual sound of an engine, the faint electric hum clear in the quiet. A small brown truck that used to be part of the town's fleet headed up toward the cannery.

A group of adults and older teenagers had been out hunting that morning, taking advantage of the growing population of deer around Wolf Branch. Humans who could no longer go to a grocery store provided the balance wolves had two hundred years before.

"There's our distraction for the day," Etan said. "Better get ready."

Chapter 2

Etan Griffith grumbled about the early mornings, having to be up and in town before the sun came up. Snow plows never had made it all the way up to the house where he grew up outside of Wolf Branch, or the house just down the road he now shared with Alex.

The frequent snow days had been a treat when he was a kid. Having to go to school nearly into summer never outweighed the pleasure of sleeping in and playing in the snow all day long.

He'd never imagined being the one who had to drive at a crawl over snowy roads to get to town to open the classroom on time, no matter how badly he wanted just a few more minutes of sleep.

Even on those mornings, the comfort and familiarity settled over Etan like a well-loved blanket as soon as he stepped through the cannery's double doors. That was the only time the huge building was silent and still.

Two rows of wide stainless steel tables ran the length of the room, with connections to the black pipes overhead dropping down every few feet. The cauldron-sized pressure canners they'd need today took up one whole wall, as did storage shelves crowded with every kitchen tool imaginable.

Deep square prep sinks and a row of commercial ranges and

ovens rounded out the space, along with more specialty machines and devices than even Etan's grandparents had known how to use.

The cannery finally started to warm up around him with a crowd of kids and adults, bringing three big deer and ten chickens from local flocks stowed in the old town truck. Despite many happy hours spent in the heat and noise of the cannery with his grandparents, Etan had never learned how to process meat.

Processing the animals down into manageable chunks was hardly his favorite thing in the world. But he certainly appreciated the quick and easy meals later on.

He and Alex both stayed out of the way when the huge band saws in the corner fired up to handle the venison. The high-pitched whir and drop was familiar from hours of helping his father and grandfather build or repair things. Watching this saw used for breaking down a deer once - knowing what that drop in the sound of the saw meant - had been enough for both Etan and Alex.

So today they busied themselves starting up the silvery barrels of the pressure canners and bringing out out heavy skillets and stock pots. All of the massive industrial strength ranges would be busy getting the meat browned and chicken stock ready.

The long, echoing space, all concrete and cinderblocks and steel surfaces, filled with chatter and the unmistakable ring of the big saw. But none of the squeaks and bangs of equipment trouble Etan remembered from his childhood. Alex and an enthusiastic group of locals had gone to work almost as soon as they'd arrived in Wolf Branch two years ago, cleaning up the abandoned building, updating every pipe and gear and nozzle.

Fresh from Chicago and leaving his engineering career behind, Alex had led the way in turning a hulking old empty building into the thriving focus and heart of their new community.

Crashing glass from the front of the building had Etan jerking his head up and around. The remains of a couple of quart jars were scattered on the floor, light from the overhead windows highlighting the jagged, sparkling bits. Jessie Estep, one of the young teenage boys from Maple Ridge, his face blazing red, ran toward the office for a broom.

Etan snorted and turned back to the pot he was filling with water.

"The only thing Alex can't replace or repair," a woman said from his other side. "I wouldn't be surprised if he figures it out, though."

"Hey Gena. He frets about that more than you've believe. Iris and her hunting party brought in a good haul."

Gena laughed, looking back toward the noisy back room. She'd been part of the group rescued from Maple Ridge back in December, the day after the nightmare raid on Wolf Branch. Her dark blonde hair shifted over her shoulders, and she was a bit shorter than Etan. He could see Gena's partner Iris, her black hair caught back in a braid that made sense with what she was demonstrating.

"She's happy as a pig in shit, as my great-grandmother would have said. The hound dogs are, too. I'm happy to sit that part out, but Iris says even city girls have to know how to cook venison to make it out here."

"The cooking part I can handle," Etan said. "I'm glad someone else wants to do the hunting."

Jessie ran back out, stopping himself so abruptly beside the broken glass than his shoes gave a harsh shriek against the concrete floor. His cheeks and ears deepened to ripe tomato red, but he shrugged and grinned at Etan and Gena before sweeping up the glass.

"How's Jessie doing?" Etan said, arranging meat forks and tongs beside the cooktop.

"Still worried about his parents, but he's not talking about them coming to get him anymore. I think seeing how many of the rest of us have tried to adjust helped a little. It's so tough not knowing."

Jessie's family had been far away when disaster struck in Maple Ridge, Wolf Branch, and the rest of the country and the world. Along with Gena's family, Alex's, and so many others. Iris was one of the few who had both parents with her.

"Classes starting up soon will help get him settled," Etan said. "Did Linda talk to you about maybe helping teach a few?"

Gena paused in sorting out tiny jars filled with the surprising number of herbs and spices they'd been able to grow in Alex's green-house. She rolled her eyes at Etan.

"Linda talked to me, yeah. I'm no poet or source of artistic prose after a few years of law school, but I can handle basic English. Same with math that isn't Alex-level. Iris beat Linda to it, though, by a few days. She painted the loveliest impressionist vision of me in a classroom surrounded by my eager pupils. I promptly suggested I'd be happy to teach, as long as she handles the art classes."

Etan grinned, wondering if he could get a look at that painting. That was how Iris's dreaming talent came out, in wild and often frightening paintings as soon as she woke. Gena knew better than Iris or anyone else what the images actually meant.

Alex often got a strong idea about the paintings, probably because he'd spent years listening to Etan's dreams in the middle of the night. Those dreams had led the two of them to give up the lives they'd loved in Chicago and venture back to these mountains.

And Etan could no longer deny how that choice had *saved* their lives, just as it had many others who'd arrived in Wolf Branch before and after them. Worldwide, chronic food shortages had weakened the distribution systems and the societies that depended on them. A genetically engineered fungus, purposely released into the corn crops so many staple foods and industries were built upon, destroyed modern food chains and populations and so much that went with them.

News sources like radio, television, and the Internet were years gone. But best guesses and dreams suggested hundreds of millions dead in North America, billions more worldwide.

"Hey Gena." Alex had returned from the meat processing room, face paler than usual under the scattering of freckles. "I think that's enough deer dismemberment for me for today. What can I help with out here?"

She grinned and handed him a thicker than normal pair of kitchen scissors.

"As soon as they finish up in there, we'll be ready for breaking the chickens down. Sounds like you're our man."

Chapter 3

Deer and chickens safely broken down, cooked up, and canned, Alex and Etan escaped the warm air of the cannery for the empty football and baseball fields next door. Idle talk over the long, difficult winter had given way to an eagerness to get started, to turn the huge expanse of cleared land over to food production.

A few Wolf Branch natives grumbled about the change, around town and at the organized - and closed - council meetings. But none of them in any meaningful or serious way.

The fields were more scenic than most, with the steep hills covered with trees rising up all around them. But the value of flat, cleared land in a mountain town was too high to ignore.

Just another growing pain for their new community, and a reluctant admission of how much things had changed. No one in the new world would honestly argue that they'd ever have need of the carefully groomed and maintained spaces once set aside for large-scale sports.

Everyone left, including the kids, worked way too hard to have need of such a diversion anyway.

After the flood of tools they'd gotten when the community garden started up, Alex knew what they'd get for much more land would outgrow their tiny shed beside the cannery. That left him and

Etan sorting through the drafty old equipment shed sitting between the baseball and football fields.

One dusty window opposite the door gave just enough light to show how carelessly everything had been thrown inside.

Alex tried to envision uses for the odd workout equipment stacked on shelves and on the concrete floor with more success than he'd expected. A bundle of flags could work for keeping seeded crops straight, along with various sizes of traffic cones and the square plots for agility training.

A slightly modified tackling sled would make short work of taking up the grass sod, with one of their alcohol-burning ATVs pulling it along.

But much as he might want to, Alex couldn't work out how they could convert the charging dummies nearly as tall as he was into anything useful.

Etan turned with his arms full of discarded practice shoes and laughed so hard he almost dropped all of them.

"The way you're standing and staring at it. Like you expect it to head butt you or something."

Alex snorted and pushed the vaguely human-shaped thing backward. It slowly rolled back, then up and toward him.

"I guess we could turn it into a scarecrow," he said. "I think we have enough uniform rags out here to outfit every one of them."

Etan dropped the shoes in a pile on the snowy grass outside, then knelt to gather up knee and elbow pads.

"I never realized how much of this stuff translated to gardening when I was wearing it."

Alex smiled, running his hands along Etan's shoulders.

"I didn't know you played football. My father wanted me to, of course. By the time I was old enough, he was used to me not living up to his expectations. Tell me about your playing days."

"Not that much to tell. I was small and fast enough to always make the team, and I had fun with it. I was better at baseball, but not good enough at either to worry about it by the time I got to college."

"Wish I'd seen you play," Alex said. He took the armful of

smelly padding, some of it rotten and crumbling, and dumped it outside beside the shoes. "I probably would have enjoyed the games a lot more. Maybe you can try on your old uniforms for me sometime."

Etan laughed and shook his head. He'd never begrudged Alex his recurring fantasies since they'd moved here, made all the more vivid by the collection of photos Etan's grandparents left in the house they now shared. He played along more often than not, to Alex's ongoing delight.

"I'd be happy to," Etan said with a wink. "If you can stand the lingering stench of adolescent boy."

By the time they finished, there was more than enough room inside to store anything short of a full-sized tractor.

"I'll let Linda know to get the word out for equipment people don't need," Alex said, leaning back with his fists pressed against his lower back. "Hopefully Walt and the rest will take pity and tell me what it's all for. My Wisconsin childhood didn't prepare me for life as a farmer as well as you'd think."

"The Council will be thrilled. More to debate and argue about."

Alex considered, but only for a few seconds. He had the strongest hunch that Etan's reluctance to join the Council was finally starting to crack.

But he still needed to go carefully.

"Iris tells me a few people on the Council are starting to have dreams about this place," he said, watching Etan's face. "The ones you had back in January about clearing all the grass out, planting the fields. Not that I'm supposed to know about that."

"Yeah? Well, good. They can thank us for emptying this shed out and help us with the rest."

Etan pulled the door closed and leaned against the shed with his arms crossed, looking up under his eyebrows at Alex.

Yep. He knew what was coming.

"They have every dream you do, E. But they have them a long time *after* you do. You're out ahead, almost every time."

Etan shrugged, but he stared down at his feet now.

"Just say it, Alex. I've been hearing it from Mom, Iris, Gena.

Half the people in Wolf Branch are afraid to bring it up to me, the other half won't shut up about it. Let's see where you stand."

Alex leaned against the wall beside him, their shoulders touching.

"You don't have to wonder about that. I'm always going to stand with you. But in this case, I'll say it. You *need* to be on the Council. *We* need to be, both of us. You're the strongest dreamer we have. We might not be finished with threats we need to see coming."

"I can't even remember the damn dreams. How pathetic is that? I'm not sure how much good I'd do them."

Alex looked away to hide his smile. They'd gone from a firm "No" to "Not right now" to "I don't belong."

Almost there.

"Most of the dreamers don't seem to remember," he said. "Iris doesn't, sometimes not even after she finishes the paintings. Not until Gena sees what they mean. You told me last year you know when I'm telling you the truth about the dreams. I think most of us are set up to work in pairs. Did you miss the part where I said we *both* need to do this?"

He reached over and took Etan's hand, the warmth reassuring against the increasingly chilly air.

"You don't realize how people trust you," Alex said. "How they *want* to follow you. They all did when we first got here, with getting the cannery up and running. That was before anyone else talked about the dreams. Whether you want to be or not, you're a leader. We need all the real leaders we can get."

Etan sighed and squeezed Alex's hand.

"Are you ever going to stop asking?"

"Yes. When you agree to go." Alex stopped and reconsidered at Etan's raised eyebrows. "Never mind, I'm not leaving you an opening that big. I'll stop asking when you actually *do* go."

Etan surprised Alex by laughing under his breath and leaning over to kiss his cheek.

"Okay, okay. I don't like it, but I'll do it for you. Can you do something for me? Wait a couple of months, for one thing. I promise I'll go, but give me some time to get ready."

"Done. They're not meeting all that often anyway. I promise I won't bug you about it again until at least June."

"Thank you. And maybe see if they can have a subcommittee or informal meeting or whatever they want to call it? If I have to walk in there in front of a huge crowd like I'm auditioning or defending a thesis, I'll never make it. I think I can handle talking to a smaller group first."

Tension he hadn't quite been aware of left Alex's shoulders and neck. He hadn't wanted to admit it with Etan so jumpy, but this wasn't a simple matter of keeping their hard-won place in their new community.

Alex had a feeling, far more deep and resonant than a hunch, that he and Etan and everyone else in Wolf Branch weren't finished fighting to survive the end of the world.

Some part of him knew more struggles waited, and wanted every possible advantage they could get.

"I'll see what I can do, sweetie," he said, pulling Etan after him and away from the shed. "If you'll take me home and figure out how to warm both of us up."

Chapter 4

Alex was as good as his word, biding his time before arranging for Etan to meet with six people instead of the full council. And none of those six would be Mary Shadrin or any of her followers.

The disturbing woman hadn't been as openly disdainful of Alex - or as obvious in her desire to be in charge of more than her own group - since the disastrous raid from Maple Ridge. But she hadn't been exactly friendly and warm, either.

Etan was still nervous when he and Alex parked outside the town hall. Etan stared at the one-story red brick building, the same one he'd seen his entire life. Concrete steps up to the white front door. Windows at even intervals around the whole thing. Cheery blue curtains hanging in each one.

The only thing that seemed to change over time was the color of those curtains and the contents of the row of stone planters out front. Etan remembered helping build them one summer when he was twelve or thirteen, and helping his grandmother plant flowers in them. This time of year, vivid purple irises shared space with cheery yellow black-eyed Susans and bunches of mums and daisies.

Etan was touched that someone cared enough to carry on that little tradition when so much had changed around them.

This wouldn't be an unruly gathering like they'd had at the high

school what felt like years ago, when half the town outed themselves as dreamers in front of the packed-full auditorium. Not even
the typical meeting Etan imagined and dreaded, with a dozen or
more people arguing around the big oval table in the main room
inside.

Even with a group well-known to him and no set agenda, he
couldn't help feeling like he was walking into a lion's den.

The only thing that gave him even the hope of going in there
was knowing he hadn't been the only one to dream of this. Everyone
else in there waiting had the dream, or slept beside someone
who had.

"You're sure it was tonight?" he said, knowing how silly it
sounded before he finished speaking.

"I'm sure, E."

Alex made no move to get out of the car or tease Etan into it. He
simply sat and waited.

Maddening.

And more than enough reason to marry Alex all over again.

"All right. I guess it's just as well I never got the chance to defend
a doctoral thesis or anything else remotely public, huh? I never
would have made it. Let's get this nightmare over with."

The room itself was a pleasant surprise, one Alex had surely
helped arrange. They weren't scattered across the big conference
room, or even crowded into one of the smaller rooms with a table.
This was more like a break room than anything else, as in a *real*
break from work rather than a refrigerator jammed into two cabinets
with a constantly dingy microwave and unreliable coffee maker in
the middle.

Several comfortable chair were tucked into a carpeted room,
with non-glaring lighting and even a television on the wall. Someone
- Etan again suspected Alex - had supplied their own bottled beer
and cider to go along with fresh fruit and a cheese plate that could
have come from a fancy grocery store in Chicago rather than entirely
from Wolf Branch.

A blonde woman who looked strange wearing something besides
hospital scrubs stood to shake his hand. Doctor Sandy Hughes,

another Wolf Branch native who'd returned back home from Chicago before the end.

"Glad to see you, Etan, Alex. I'm here for you more than the Council. Moral support and all."

Right behind Sandy was Linda Burns, the high school teacher who'd helped so much in getting the cannery up and running. Her gray hair was caught up in its usual unruly bun.

"I'm not officially on the Council, Etan. Just here to back you up."

"I'm relieved to have at least two people on my side." Etan winked at the two women, waiting for Alex to elbow him. Right on cue, he did. "Three I suppose, even though Alex did drag me here."

"I love how he accuses me," Alex said, "without mentioning that he drove us here. Should I go get the others?"

"We're all here," a deep, rich voice said from behind them.

Etan turned to see George Light, a former preacher from eastern Virginia who'd arrived with many of his congregation not long after Sandy had. He towered over Etan and even Alex, and his dark brown face held a broad, welcoming smile.

Harry Mullins, a local businessman who'd finally given up his blue or black or gray suits for jeans and flannel shirts, followed behind George. He'd even grown a bit of a neatly trimmed beard, streaked with gray like his thick brown hair.

Harry had pushed for the Council in the first place, and Etan's more cynical side might have suspected a profit or power motivation in the past. But Harry had also admitted his dreams in public that night in the high school auditorium, making it safe for dozens of others to do the same.

Etan wanted to cry with relief when Iris and Gena walked in and closed the door behind them. Ever since he'd met the two of them - the night his mother had organized a massive church feed to welcome everyone who'd survived imprisonment up on Maple Ridge - Etan had felt at home and comfortable with Iris and Gena.

He didn't quite feel relaxed, but a good bit of his fear of walking into some kind of interrogation room had eased by the time the greetings were over and everyone finally found a seat.

Alex spoke before Etan had a chance to worry about what to say himself.

"We all know Wolf Branch doesn't run on anything like parliamentary procedure. Our community is doing as well as it is because so many of us are running on dreams. Our dreams, our partner's dreams. That's how Etan and I got here, why we left Chicago. We're here in this room because Etan's dreams seem to run ahead of everyone else's. Months ahead."

He turned to Etan, eyebrows raised. *Ready to talk?*

Etan was surprised to find he was.

"I was afraid of getting into all of this, and I still am. But I think Alex is right that these dreams work in pairs. For most of us, anyway. If whatever happens inside my head can help get all of us ready, maybe we won't have…as many surprises."

He'd thought he could just say it.

Another attack like last year.

But…

Seeing Iris and Gena, knowing the hell they'd gone through. Remembering Linda and especially Sandy taking care of him and his family after that awful explosion.

The way his mother hid her face against his chest that night, the next morning, and more than once in the long days that followed.

Simple words weren't always so simple.

Linda rescued him before he could catch his breath.

"We wouldn't have been nearly as ready if it weren't for you and Alex and all your hard work. The cannery and the garden and everything you've both taught us, that made all the difference when the outside world tore itself apart."

Sandy nodded. "We're sitting here in a room with lights and food and even this fine beer because of you. We have a hospital with lights and fresh water that we wouldn't have otherwise. You're already leaders in Wolf Branch, Etan. If you're willing to do more, we'd only be lucky. And grateful."

Etan stared at his feet, fighting his desire to argue with everything both women had said, but only for a second. He looked up at everyone's nods and smiles, and he couldn't ignore his sense of being in the right place. On the right path.

On the same path as the love of his life, who pretty much *had* dragged him into this room, but with damn good reason.

"Okay," Etan said. "I'm not sure what I can offer, what we both can. But I want to try. What's next?"

Harry leaned forward, fingers knitted together between his knees. Etan managed not to smile when he noticed mud around the cuffs of his jeans, a far cry from those spotless suits.

"I don't mean to sound like I'm doubting you, Etan. Just trying to understand what might be happening. What kinds of things are you dreaming about before the rest of us do?"

Etan was afraid he was going to freeze up again, trying to drag words out of himself to explain what he still didn't understand. He suspected Alex had known something was going to happen before the raiders attacked.

But he'd never yet worked up the nerve to ask more about what, and how.

And why Alex hadn't told him.

"Etan doesn't usually remember his dreams," Alex said, his words getting out just ahead of Gena's.

"Iris hardly ever knows what her dreams are until she finishes the paintings. Sometimes not even then."

Etan caught the flash of humor and recognition between Alex and Gena, and he was nothing but grateful. And he remembered the hint Alex had already given him.

"They're right," he said. "None of this works without Alex as my witness. One thing I remember is everyone seemed to decide all at once to get those fields planted around the high school. Alex told me I dreamed of that for a few months before anyone else mentioned it."

Harry nodded, lips pressed together in a tight smile. "My wife Cindy said the same thing, but only a few days before we started."

"*Witness* is a lovely way to put it, Etan," Iris said, smiling at Gena. "I felt like that the first time Gena saw one of my paintings.

That I finally had a witness to whatever makes that come through my fingers. What are you dreaming now? Anything new?"

"I'll be more honest than I want to," Etan said. "This is one big reason I hesitated so long. I don't know how to answer that even though I *have* the dreams. Maybe if Alex explains what he hears, I'll remember more."

Alex grinned. "This one's easy, then. Over the past couple of weeks you talk about gathering more supplies, while we still have vehicles that work well enough to get us outside where we've already looked. Going out to get things like eyeglasses, old solid-state computer drives, things we can't make that will last a long time. But the newest thing is paper."

Sandy pulled out her tiny spiral notebook that she was never without.

"You mean like this?" she said. "Or printer paper?"

"Everything and anything you can find," Etan said. "Talking did make it clear in my mind. Journals, notebooks, all of it. Pens and pencils too, for as long as they'll last. We need to start writing the dreams down, recording them. I don't know why, but it's going to be vital. We can figure out how to make paper and even pencils some-day, but for now we have to get all we can find."

"That makes sense," George Light said, staring up at the ceiling. "We've been keeping the dreams secret outside the Council, as best we could at least. We'd be able to verify things then, more like a prophecy than a prediction."

"You sound like you want to start a religion," Etan said. "That's the last thing we need. How many of the problems that made every-thing worse at the end were because of religion?"

Etan tried to keep himself from groaning out loud. What had he just said, to a former preacher of all people?

"I'm sorry, George. I shouldn't have said that."

George laughed, deep and loud, holding his huge hands up toward Etan. "No, the whole point of this is we *want* to hear what you have to say. Both of you. We need to hear it, and not the polite version. If you're dreaming so far out ahead of us, things like this could be crucial."

Iris shrugged. "Most of us agree with you, that's the hard part. What happened on Maple Ridge started out with a kind of twisted religion. Going by what little we know of how things fell apart, different beliefs about the end times killed as many people as sickness and starvation did. But we need some kind of motivation for people to listen. To follow us. What we have to say won't always be as easy as gathering paper."

"We've had more arguments about the food stores already," Linda said, fussing with loose ends of her gray hair. "Some of it from within the Council from what I've heard, and not just Mary Shadrin. We'll have to find a better way to work together to have a chance."

Etan didn't have to look at Alex to know he was biting his tongue, dying to say something. He could feel how tense Alex's leg was against his own, could just about *hear* his agitation.

"What are you wanting to say, Alex?"

"I don't want to be an asshole, but if we have to set you up as a prophet, that's what we need to do. I hated what happened in Maple Ridge and everywhere else. But we can't have gone through so much hell to get here and let everything fall apart again. If people will follow the Great Prophet Etan and that lets us survive, then that's who you need to be."

Etan did groan then, closing his eyes for a second. Not only because this was what he'd been afraid of. Because the words and the ideas sounded true.

They *felt* true, no matter how much he might dislike them.

"I don't know if I can agree to that, not right now. I have no idea how to do *any* of this, much less create a new religion. I'm scared to death of making a hard situation worse."

This time Alex didn't hesitate.

"How could you make it worse? You don't even remember the dreams, E. If anyone should be nervous, it's me. I'm the one who has to figure out what's got you so stirred up in the middle of the night and try to remember it all."

"You always do, Alex."

"Exactly," he said with a grin. "What are you so worried about then? Especially if I start writing them down on all this paper we need to find."

Etan realized he'd finally learned to recognize when it was time to stop resisting, even if he still wanted to. Another of those scratchy, dissonant pieces inside of him moved the tiniest bit at Alex's words.

Shifting into harmony.

"I won't make any promises," he said, smiling to soften the words. "But I'll do my best. Let's figure out what comes next."

Chapter 5

ONE THING ALEX hadn't counted on when they joined the Council was Etan deciding to move a few months later.

Everyone on the Council lived in town, either in a few scattered houses or in brick apartment buildings built well over a hundred years ago. All of them within walking distance of each other, the cannery, and the town hall.

That all made perfect sense to Alex, and he couldn't think of a real reason for arguing about it. The apartment was lovely, for one thing.

One floor up from Iris and Gena, a few blocks from Etan's mother Laura. A bright, sprawling space, with gleaming original wood floors and window seats, and a big, well-designed kitchen.

Four bedrooms seemed like far more space than they'd ever need, but Alex wasn't bothered by that. He knew in his heart, as strongly as he ever had, that their future would include children to fill up all that space in the beat of a sweet little heart.

This building had a modern boiler in the basement like the others did, one Alex and his dedicated crew had updated to run on what they could grow. No more shivering in an old, under-insulated house while they waited for a creaky wood stove to get going every morning.

After the heartbreaking departure from their shoebox apartment in Chicago overlooking Lake Michigan, he'd never imagined a move of a few miles would bother him.

But Alex had come to love their little house hidden away in the woods more than he'd realized.

He couldn't explain it to himself, much less to Etan. Maybe because it wasn't just one thing.

It was the memory of their first day in Wolf Branch, when Etan's mother had welcomed them with chocolate chip cookies, a fully stocked kitchen, and a bottle of bourbon. Many walks just down the road to Laura and Connor's house for spectacular meals in Connor's outdoor kitchen.

He and Etan learning they did have a place here, that they'd actually be needed and happy. Settling in where Etan's grandparents Anne and Evan had spent so many wonderful years, surrounded by all their books and photographs.

Alex had even come to love that creaky wood stove, the routine and satisfaction of heating the house with his own labor rather than touching a screen. He would miss the way he could adjust the scent of the fire depending on how he selected and arranged the wood almost as much as the aroma and taste of apple cider heated on top.

He leaned against the curved archway in the heart of the house, the now-empty library where first Evan and Anne, then he and Etan had spent so many hours reading and studying and learning.

Seeing shelves Etan's grandfather and father had carefully built left without a single book or photo broke Alex's heart. But the hundreds of volumes had been too valuable in helping all of Wolf Branch get ready and have a chance at survival to leave them here.

Neither he nor Etan could abandon the pictures for far more sentimental reasons.

All the books and photos, the burgundy wingback chairs, and the matching ottoman waited in a jumble in the apartment, along with the antiquated but still functional computers. Even Anne's fuzzy pink blanket had made the trip.

Alex had agonized over the contents of Connor's secret hiding place, the tiny door above one top shelf. He'd finally taken the journals written in Evan's hand and built a secret place for them in the apartment, in the bedroom that would be their new library.

The message sent from a man who'd died before they could have met would stay safe as long as Alex lived.

He heard Etan's steps echoing in the empty living room behind him. Alex held out his arm, smiling at the way Etan still fit perfectly against him after five years.

How well must Etan's grandparents have fit after knowing each other for nearly eighty years?

Alex hoped to find out.

"This is hitting you almost as hard as leaving Chicago, isn't it?" Etan said, slipping his arms around Alex.

"Almost. I thought we'd be in this house the rest of our lives, you know?"

"I know. I'm sorry, Alex. I didn't realize-"

Alex turned to face Etan, brushing his hair back from his forehead.

"No, it all makes sense, moving into town. We might have plenty of power from Maple Ridge now, but we can't do a whole lot for these old roads. It was bad enough trying to get around this past winter. I'll love it there, too, once I get settled in. As long as you're there, it's home."

"Leaving Wisconsin and your family didn't bother you like this, did it?"

Alex laughed and pulled Etan close.

"Not even a little. I hope they're as okay as anyone can be out there now. But my life didn't start until I left. My family is right here."

Etan leaned up for a kiss Alex was happy to provide. A kiss that quickly made Alex wish the bed was still here, or at least some of the furniture. Hell, a blanket, or maybe a beach towel would do.

They were both laughing when they stopped to catch their breath.

"Too bad we can't take the tub," Etan said. "We've had some damn good times there."

"I can't imagine how we'd move a stone soaking tub built into the wall and the floor, much less get it up four flights of stairs. I doubt even the apartment's service elevator would manage. We'll have to make do without it."

"That rickety old hand crank thing you keep telling everyone is safe? I wasn't thrilled with putting our furniture on it."

"Worked just fine," Alex said with a grin. "And saved us lugging a couch up four flights."

They laughed together, ending up in another kiss. Etan grabbed Alex's hand and pulled him unresisting toward the bathroom.

"That last load of books will be fine out in the yard for a while. Time enough for one more memory."

PART II
WITH NEW LIFE

Chapter 6

Even after a year, Etan's favorite thing about the apartment was the first thing he'd noticed. All the morning light. Not in their bedroom, thank goodness. That was tucked away on the north side of the building.

But the kitchen and the living room and the tiny little dining nook were all on the east side, set under lovely tall windows. Neither their apartment in Chicago or the house here had much light at all, and definitely not in the morning.

Here the early daylight streamed in from the time the sun cleared the mountains circling Wolf Branch until it set on the other side, gleaming off the aged hardwood floors. The natural light was a lovely change of pace.

The high ceilings kept the rooms from overheating even when summer was in full swing. And the winter sun had supplemented the ornate antique radiators and sleek modern baseboards quite nicely.

His mother worked her magic in this new place just like she had when they first arrived in Wolf Branch more than four years ago. She didn't have nearly the resources, with the grocery store getting its last delivery years earlier, and the liquor store longer ago than that.

But she'd still managed to stock up their kitchen with spring produce fresh from the community garden that now thrived on the old football and baseball fields, Iris's venison, and fresh baked bread. She'd helped figure out how to arrange their furniture in the larger space, and even where to hang several of the photos from the old house.

A quiet conversation about how much the images mattered now that printed photographs had slipped into history added more ritual than routine to what seemed like a simple task.

She'd helped Etan and Alex transform one of the bedrooms on the same bright side of the apartment into a wonderful library, larger than what they'd had in his grandparents' house. Anne and Evan still lingered, in their chairs and photos and even their ancient computers.

Still providing the guidance that had already proven so essential in getting Wolf Branch through the first pains of the end of the world.

Etan smiled at the sight of Alex curled up on the same charcoal gray couch he'd brought with him when he moved into Etan's apartment years ago. The sturdy canvas had held up beautifully after so many hours and miles. He leaned over the back and put his arms around Alex's shoulders.

"Good morning, handsome."

"Good morning to you."

Etan drew back, surprised at the odd sound in his husband's voice. His expression didn't help. Alex was smiling, but he had one eyebrow raised.

"What's wrong?"

"Not a thing. Sit down, I'll get you breakfast. The tea's still hot."

Alex put eggs, toast, and greenhouse strawberries in front of him before he sat down. The spring mornings were still chilly enough that Etan curled his fingers around the warm mug full of dark holly tea.

A few dedicated caffeine addicts had finally managed to get yaupon hollies to grow in the greenhouse the year before, and the resulting brew was more treasured than moonshine. Dreamers and their witnesses especially appreciated the energy boost after a long night, even though their honeybee colonies were too few and precious to gather honey from just yet.

Alex sipped at his own mug with that strange little smile until Etan rolled his eyes and sighed.

"What is going on with you this morning?"

Alex shook his head. "Just wondering how you slept last night."

Etan chewed the last bit of toast, trying to remember. He didn't feel tired as if he'd had a nightmare. He couldn't have been too restless for Alex to be up so much earlier.

Etan felt great, in fact, better than he had for a long time.

"Did we… You didn't violate me in my sleep, did you?"

"Not exactly," Alex said with a soft laugh. "Someone did, but not me."

Etan grunted, pushing his plate away.

"What the hell are you talking about? Just tell me, I'm not in the mood for a guessing game."

"Okay," Alex said, still with that odd smile. "You were dreaming about sex, all right. Sex with Iris and Gena."

"Oh come on. That's a load of shit."

Alex tilted his head to the side.

"Okay, then. Tell me I just lied to you. Tell me what I just said didn't feel true."

"No," Etan said, wishing he *could* argue for some reason. But he did feel that little click of truth, along with a distant, echoing excitement. "You don't lie about much of anything, even when you should."

"You were noisy enough that I had an idea what was going on. You sound pretty much the same making love asleep as when you're awake, by the way. When you finally woke up, you told me you were with the two of them. So you could have children."

Etan stared up at the speckled white ceiling, trying not to let his upset show. That was one of the losses Alex felt the most keenly, enough that it had broken Etan's heart. One of their *someday* plans had been to go to the university in Chicago, to have their genes combined so they could father children that would belong to both of them.

The world had ended before *someday* ever came. Even if that were still possible, if anyone was left alive who knew how, Chicago was several days dangerous journey to the northwest.

"You know I don't want kids if they're not yours too, Alex."

"I do know, I understand. We might have missed our chance at that, sweetie."

"So that's done then," Etan said, pouring more tea for both of them. "We're not having kids."

"Look around you, E, pay attention. There aren't enough of us, not by a long shot. We can't afford to be sentimental about this."

"Well, I don't want to, not without you."

"Sometimes I wonder if your brain only works when you're asleep. What makes you think you'd be raising them without me? Do you really think I wouldn't love a kid that came from you?"

"I'm sure you would, Alex, but I wanted them with you. That was the whole point. You matter more to me than propagating the species."

Alex leaned back in his chair and crossed his arms.

"You're gonna have to reconsider that point of view. We all have to step up on that one. None of this is going to matter if we die out after a couple of generations. We've been on the Council long enough, heard enough stories, to know we have to have the dreamers if we're going to survive. You *know* that. Whatever causes this has to be passed on."

Somewhere deep in his heart, and in the warm trembling in his belly, Etan knew arguing was useless. Alex hadn't just brought this up out of the blue. So far, Etan's dreams had never been wrong.

Having children now, whatever the means, scared him to his bones.

"But I don't have to pass it on, Alex. I'm not going to."

"Yeah, *you* do. Especially you. Listen to what I'm saying, and remember you *dreamed* about this. No one else here has the same kinds of dreams you do. Maybe no one else on this empty planet. You're months or more ahead of everyone else, sometimes a year. You usually see more than anyone else, too. Whatever gift or curse you have is too important to not try and preserve it."

Etan got up and walked over to the window, his precious tea forgotten. The cherry, plum, and apricot trees in the sheltered square between four of the apartments would be full of flowers in a few weeks, with rows of greens planted in between. Several stacks of honeybee boxes - the winter homes to several of their precious surviving colonies - clustered together in the middle.

For a brief, disorienting second, Etan saw it full of children, heard their laughter.

His children. Alex's.

Their children.

He shook his head.

"I'm not the only one who's not thinking, jackass," he said. "If it weren't for you, no one would ever know about these crazy dreams. They might happen inside my own skull, but I can't remember them. How pathetic is that, Alex? Such a supposedly great resource, and I'm the only one who can't use it. It doesn't mean a damn thing without you. Nothing does."

Etan heard Alex get up. He was torn between wanting him to leave the room, leave him alone to fume and get more agitated, and wanting Alex to put his arms around his waist and comfort him somehow.

He sighed and leaned back into his husband's warmth. As usual, Alex made the right choice when Etan couldn't even begin to think.

"Well, that's the other part of the dream, E, the really interesting part," he said in a low voice, his lips against Etan's ear. "You told me we're both going to make love to Iris, and we're both going to make love to Gena. Both of us. Apparently when you're asleep, you do appreciate me, or at least you appreciate that I have something worth passing along too."

Etan turned, putting his arms around Alex's shoulders. That touch fractured some kind of mental wall, revealing a glint from deep down inside his mind. He rarely remembered anything about his dreams at all, at least not the prophecy dreams.

Right now he saw, he *felt*, everything that was going to happen.

"Both of us, at the same time," Etan whispered. "We'll be with them together."

"That's what I've been trying to tell you, but you won't close your runaway mouth long enough to listen to me. I can't think of a better way to solve this problem for all four of us, can you?"

Alex stopped Etan's mouth, and his thoughts, with a kiss.

"We'll both be with both of them, together," Alex said against Etan's lips. "You said we'd do that so we wouldn't know who the father was. So the father would be *both* of us. You said we'd do that so neither of us would be alone."

"I've never even been with a woman," Etan said, pulling Alex against him. "Much less two."

"I have." Alex laughed under his breath. "Well, one at a time, at least. It's not all that complicated. I'll be right there with you."

Alex kissed him again, then moved to Etan's ear, his throat.

"Will they even agree to all of this?" Etan said.

"I think Iris will have the same dream, don't you? She seems to be the one closest behind you. Gena will know as soon as Iris does."

"They'll probably be the ones to bring it up." Etan gasped when Alex bit the sensitive flesh where his neck joined his shoulder. "Neither of them strikes me as the shy type."

"You wouldn't be so damn shy if you'd just listen to me a little more often. Come back to bed."

Etan followed gladly, amazed at how clearly everything was coming back to him. He remembered all of it - the first time he'd ever recalled a dream like this.

The four of them would be awkward at first, himself more than the others. His touch would be hesitant, so uncertain, but having Alex with him would push that away. The four of them would find a rhythm, a comfort and a passion he never could have imagined.

As he was in everything else, Alex was the key.

He unbuttoned Etan's shirt, following the lines of his fingers with his mouth. He sat on the bed, pushing Etan's jeans down over his hips.

"It's not just that you haven't been with a woman, is it?" he said, so close that Etan strained toward the heat of his breath. "You've never been inside someone else, not like that."

Alex took him into his mouth then, and Etan groaned.

"Just your mouth," Etan whispered. "Just your sweet fucking mouth."

Alex stood and moved Etan's hands to his own shirt. He kissed him while Etan fumbled with the buttons. Naked, Alex moved onto the bed, pulling them both down together.

"I want you to, Etan. I want to be your first."

Etan drew back.

"You don't… Have you ever?"

Alex smiled, nodding.

"A few times when I was a kid, yeah. Around the same time I was with women. That was all before I met you."

"I don't want you to be uncomfortable," Etan said.

What Etan wanted was to be done with talking. He wanted to be done with thinking and everything else besides the two of them in this warm bed, at least for a while.

Alex laughed. "Just hush and listen to me, stop arguing with me. I *want* to, with you. Right now. I don't want your first time to be with someone else."

Alex moved Etan's hand down along his body, into the heat between them.

"Let me be your first," he whispered, moving against Etan's hand.

"I don't want to hurt you, Alex."

"Have I ever hurt you?"

"No, you never have. It's always good with you."

"Remember your first time then. Your first *good* time."

Etan closed his eyes, letting that deep, hot memory move through his body. Until that night, sex had felt like something he should do, a requirement. A chore on a list, or a way to relax enough to get to sleep.

Alex changed the chore into a necessity. Making love turned into a craving as deep as the need for food, for air, and that hadn't lessened over the years.

"You were my first good time, Alex."

Alex shifted, moving until Etan's hips were between his legs.

"Do what I did, then. Take your time, go slow. We don't have anywhere else to be today. You're not going to hurt me. Don't you want me?"

For the first time, the first time since he'd started being honest with himself about such things many years ago, Etan did want to be inside of another person.

He wanted to move inside of Alex, to push toward him.

He wanted to try to be part of him.

"Yes," he whispered, his breath speeding up along with his heartbeat. "I want you. I want every part of you."

"Then take me. Take me the same way I took you. I want to feel you inside me."

Etan laughed, the intensity of his body's demands making him dizzy. He took Alex's mouth first, exploring every wet, warm fold like they'd never kissed before.

Their first time together surged into his mind like a vision, like the strongest dream he'd ever had.

His mouth, Alex's mouth, that's what they always started with. No one else had ever turned Etan on so much, like Alex was starving to death for every inch of him. He understood where that fierce appetite came from now.

Etan drew back and looked at Alex's flushed face, nearly lost in his memory. Their roles reversed, both of their bodies unknown and so much younger. Every motion and taste a revelation.

So many years, so much passion between them only made this sweeter.

Like his dreams of the two of them with Iris and Gena, his movements were hesitant at first. Unsure.

But Etan caught the pace of his lover, and he knew that rhythm was a part of him, a song he'd known since the first day he'd looked into Alex's eyes.

The same song that would sing new life into the empty world.

Chapter 7

Alex happily reacquired his lifelong habit of walking everywhere he needed to go. He'd thought that simple activity was lost to him once they'd left Chicago. Distance from their first house in Wolf Branch made it impractical, and often impossible in bad weather.

But their apartment changed the rhythm of their lives in more good ways than bad.

And just like in Chicago, walking in early summer after a long winter was pure joy. The sun wasn't yet fierce enough to force him into long sleeves and a hat, with commercial sunscreen long expired. The early harvests coming into the cannery had eased enough to give him and Etan short days. They'd be glad for the break once the hectic late summer and autumn harvests rolled in.

The two of them turned the corner into the courtyard behind their building to see a bigger crowd enjoying the late afternoon weather there than at the closed-in cannery.

Alex spotted Etan's mother Laura, Linda Burns, and Iris and Gena, all working around the new grape vines. Walt Colley beside the beehives towered over all of them, standing out even more with his white beekeeper's hat covering his face.

Neither Alex nor Etan had mentioned the dreams of Iris and

Gena, not least of all because neither of them had any idea how they possibly could. The dreams continued, though, almost every night.

Neither of them minded the pleasurable waking results of so much sleeping time focused on lovemaking.

Walt bent over one of the hives for a few seconds, and Alex was glad to see him slide the thin wooden cover back into place. He didn't mind the bees at all himself. In fact, he was predictably fascinated by the way they constructed and maintained their homes. Natural structural engineers.

But Etan's grip on his hand loosened when Walt pulled his hat off and turned around. Etan had never been comfortable around the honeybees or carpenter bees or bumblebees that helped keep their food supply healthy.

"Hey Walt," Alex called. "How's it going in there?"

"Hey there Alex. Etan. Just got the girls all settled in after a good checkup. Queens setting plenty of new brood, all through every one of the hives. We should have enough for the new colonies out by the cannery before it gets too hot."

Walt slipped the hat and face net under one arm so he could swallow up Alex's and then Etan's hands in his huge paw.

"I'm glad to hear that," Etan said. "We might have honey for our tea before too much longer."

Walt nodded, a grin on his long, friendly face.

"Why sure, I don't see why not. Once we have a bunch of colonies in good shape, they'll make more than enough to share with us."

Etan's mother joined them, trying to wrangle her blonde and silver curls back under her hat. Laura didn't seem quite as young as before Etan's father died, but she still looked closer to forty than nearly sixty.

"I'm just hoping for mead to go along with the wine we'll have before long," she said. "The vines are training up just fine. Did you two know Gena worked a couple of summers in the vineyards over near Hidden Springs?"

Gena stood a few steps away, Iris close beside her. They had their heads close together, clearly watching Etan and Alex. Iris's cheeks were flushed; Gena only seemed curious.

He would have bet a large sum of now-useless money that Iris had caught up with Etan's dreams. And that they were just as unsure of how to approach the whole thing as he and Etan were.

"I didn't know we had any vintners among us," Alex said, smiling at Gena. "We just need someone to crack the code on bourbon."

Gena took the hint and joined them.

"I wouldn't say I'm a vintner," she said, rolling her eyes. "I mainly helped out with the vines and carried things around. I *will* volunteer for tasting whatever we come up with. Laura might need a little help."

Iris walked up, still flushed but looking Alex, then Etan in the eye.

"I don't know if it's up to your bourbon standard, Alex," she said. "But a few folks from Maple Ridge do amazing things with maple syrup and a little bit of mash."

Alex didn't need Etan's dreams or the pre-memories Etan's grandmother had. Iris had just led Gena to the next step between the four of them.

The patterns of the bees in the air, the play of the breeze across his skin, even the shape of the wispy clouds overhead let him know his life was about to change.

All of their lives were.

Gena smiled at Iris, then at Alex.

"I'm not making any promises, but we still had a bottle or two left last time I checked. We're about ready to head upstairs if you'd like to give us your expert opinion."

Etan spoke before Alex had a chance to.

"We're in. Our beer and cider isn't half bad, but I'd guess any whiskey will be good after a couple of years without."

As they followed Iris and Gena, Alex caught Etan's mother watching. Her proud and somehow mischievous smile told him all he needed to know about Laura's opinion of the whole situation.

And for whatever strange reason, his mother-in-law's smile finally brought Alex's nervousness front and center. He reached for Etan's hand, and the answering tight grip let him know he wasn't alone in that.

Iris and Gena's apartment on the third floor had the same layout as theirs. Kitchen by the door, dining room and living room by the windows. If anything, their furniture was more eclectic and colorful.

Alex was too caught up in the paintings hung on all the walls to pay much attention to anything else. He'd seen them before on brief visits, but today the shapes, the movement, captured nearly all of his attention. One in particular, full of inverted gray tornadoes, seemed to twist and shift even though he knew it couldn't be.

He was surprised when Iris handed him a clear shot glass full of amber liquid.

"Not much left that they made from corn," she said, holding her own glass up to the sunlight. "They're working on a wheat version now."

Etan and Gena held glasses, and they were clearly waiting on Alex. He turned away from the extraordinary paintings.

"To friends," Gena said. "And to the future."

The whiskey was as smooth as any bourbon, with the taste of maple but barely any sweetness.

"If we can keep making this," Alex said, "we might just survive."

Iris glanced at Gena, and Alex heard his own words echoing in his mind. Whatever caused this, the dreamers and the witnesses, had to be passed along. They'd just have to get past feeling shy and awkward and nervous.

"I'm going to guess you've had the same dreams I have," Iris said. Her cheeks were red, but her voice was clear and steady. "About the four of us."

"For a few weeks now, yeah," Etan said. "We didn't... It didn't make sense to try to explain it until you had them, too."

"Well, no." Gena smiled, holding up the bottle with the whiskey, then refilling everyone's glasses. "It's not exactly an easy thing to put into words. Even when it makes this much sense."

Alex chewed his lip, trying to figure out how to put his thoughts into words until the second he opened his mouth. Unfortunately, speaking got harder instead of easier as he went

"This sounds strange coming from me, I know. I did move here with Etan, we both turned our lives upside down because of what he dreamed. But is this… Are we all just following along because we feel like we have to? Or is this something you want to do? With us, I mean."

Iris stepped closer to him, laughing under her breath. She touched his lips with her fingertips. One thing Alex didn't have to doubt was the tingle that lit up his entire body at her touch.

"We invited you, remember? Having kids was always for *someday* for me, I'll admit. Mainly because I had no idea how it would happen short of a doctor's office, you know? Now, though, meeting you two, getting to know you. We can't get away from all the talk of population crash and having babies. But even without that, you and Etan are the ones I'd *want* to do this with. Okay?"

"Iris and I heard all about the *inescapable biological imperative* on Maple Ridge," Gena said. "We know perfectly well how that can be abused. Better than most, I hope. That's not what this is. I can't think of anyone better than my two best guy friends. You'll both be wonderful dads."

The last one to speak was the one Alex most needed to hear from.

Etan smiled at Alex, tears standing in his eyes. "You know I've wanted kids with you since we first met. I never imagined finding other people I'd want to share that with. I'm glad we're all here."

Alex held up his glass this time, waiting for the others to do the same.

"To family, then," he said. "In every form that might take."

"I need to show you something," Iris said, grabbing Alex's hand. "A painting I've been waiting years to understand."

The bedroom was night and day to Etan and Alex's. Rather than a queen bed with comfortable but ordinary dark sheets and blankets, this king-sized bed looked soft and inviting. A purple padded head-board backed up pillows in several shades, and a matching comforter looked thick enough to sleep on by itself.

On the wall opposite the bed, Alex saw the painting.

He would have sworn it was a digital frame if he'd seen it a few years before, not a flat painting. The sensation of motion was strong in the thick brushstrokes of green in the background, the carefully arranged patterns of red, yellow, black, and brown.

Those colorful markings ranged from the four ovals in the middle, not much bigger than his palm, out to smaller ones that matched, surrounding and completing the circle they created together.

"That's us," he said without thinking. The same way he understood Etan's dreams. "And our children."

"I *knew* you'd see it, Alex," Gena said, her eyes bright. "Iris painted this years ago. Before we met you two."

Alex's heart knew before his mind understood.

This was the family they would bring into this strange, broken world.

"It's beautiful," Etan said. "Did you know what it was, Iris?"

"Not until Gena saw it," Iris said. "Just as fast as Alex did. I didn't even know I was painting my dreams before then."

"Did you know it was us?" Alex said. "When we met up on Maple Ridge?"

Gena tilted her head to the side, looking at the painting, then at him.

"I knew you'd be important, that we'd know you for a long time. I wasn't sure until the dreams started. Did you know that day?"

Alex laughed, relieved he finally felt more excited than nervous.

"Sounds about like how I felt. I knew you'd be important, but I didn't know why."

"I'd say this is pretty damn important," Etan said. "Assuming we get through whatever comes next."

He and Alex had talked, probably way too much, about how this moment might go.

Would they invite the women upstairs to their place? Cook dinner, give them gifts, all in some kind of effort to prove they were good enough providers?

Or would the women invite them down here, all flirtation and seduction, both meeting them at the door wearing some sexy slip of a dress?

Neither one held a candle to the reality he felt surrounding him now.

And none of those dating rituals made sense, not here. None of them were looking for partners, or even lovers. Nothing as cold and clinical as sperm donors, either.

Something different, then.

Their own kind of family.

"If we're both having the dreams," Iris said, reaching for Alex's hand, "I think that means the time is right. Would waiting and trying to plan something dramatic make any difference?"

"I think we'd all be a hell of a lot more nervous," Alex said.

In the laughter, the reminder of the friendship they already shared, Gena stepped into his arms, Iris into Etan's.

Gena felt so small and fragile to him, like he might break her if he squeezed too hard. But her arms were strong around his waist, and he found she fit him in a way no one besides Etan ever had.

Alex looked into his husband's eyes and saw the same surprise and relief there.

Then Alex focused on Gena, on the way she seemed to dance with him to music he couldn't hear, but felt in every part of himself.

The music of their shared future.

Chapter 8

ALL THE DREAMS and wondering and talking in the world couldn't have prepared Etan for Iris, then Gena, announcing they were pregnant. Alex's laughter and hugs all around didn't quite cover up the tears of joy in his blue eyes.

Etan's tears didn't come until hours later, until he and Alex were at home alone. In their home that was about to change forever.

While they wouldn't be husbands to the mothers of their children, or even boyfriends, both men were more than happy to take on the roles of expectant fathers. Helping around the apartment, bringing in the craved food they could still get. Attending appointments with Doctor Sandy, who was delighted to report that all seemed well.

Etan's sweetest fatherly duty so far was having his mother Laura and Iris's parents over for dinner at Iris and Gena's apartment to share the news. The excitement of three grandparents-to-be helped make up the five who were missing, and missed.

Laura even managed to bring Etan's own grandparents in on the celebration. She stated quite pointedly (and more than once) that his and Alex's wedding rings were looking dreadfully scuffed and dirty. That old Charlie Kennedy had made her promise to bring them in from time to time to get cleaned up and polished back into presentable shape.

When she returned them a few days later, each white gold band held a deep green stone set within the facets and angles. Two of the four Anne had worn on her engagement ring for so many years.

Charlie had set each of the other two stones into thin bands perfectly fitted for Iris and Gena. The last request in Anne and Evan's will, and Anne's last vision brought into reality at last.

Whether it was a real shift in the lives of everyone in Wolf Branch, or simply the four of them focusing inward, the whole community seemed calm, waiting. These babies would be the first born to Dreamers and Witnesses since they understood what those roles were.

And the first in Wolf Branch since the end of the old world.

The Council meetings and even everyone's dreams slowed to background noise. Nothing but static compared to the stirring of new life.

Both babies quickened and moved as summer gave way to autumn.

Etan's mood cooled along with the weather, though he tried to keep the change to himself. He wasn't afraid or starting to regret the oncoming change in their lives. He wasn't even worried about not knowing what to do with a newborn, not yet. He and Alex planned to stay with Iris and Gena for the first few weeks, with frequent grandparent attendance, so they could make mistakes and learn and finally figure it out together.

Yet something dragged at him, a fear he couldn't define.

His dreams didn't give him any insight, at least not that Alex could catch. Nothing more than restless nights that kept both of them from sleeping. Etan knew Alex was worried too, even when he joked it was just practice for pacing the floor with an infant.

But with all of Sandy's tools and experience still saying everything was normal, all they could do was sleep when they could.

And wait.

One afternoon halfway through October Etan jumped at the knock on the door, not sure where he was for several seconds. He'd been dreaming, a normal dream of their shoebox apartment in Chicago. The only remarkable part of that dream was how much he still missed those simple, silly days he and Alex had together before everything fell apart.

Another knock, this one more urgent. He sat up slowly, pulling his mind and body bit by bit away from that far-off life. This was the gray sofa Alex had brought with him, but the view out of the windows was mountains rather than an endless lake.

He was in Wolf Branch. He and Alex both were. This was their much larger apartment right in the middle of a much smaller town.

"Hang on," he called, finally getting to his feet. He'd been sleeping far more deeply than he usually did in the afternoon.

He opened the door to see Gena with her hand raised to knock again. Her face was pale, but she had bright spots on her cheeks.

"Hey Gena. Come on in."

"I'm sorry, I didn't mean to wake you," she said. Most of the grogginess left Etan at the anxious tone of her voice. "I think I need help."

"What's wrong? Come sit down."

"I think I need to go to the hospital." Tears stood in her eyes. "I wouldn't bother you, but Iris is at the high school. I'm bleeding, Etan. Pretty bad."

Cold flooded his whole body, and a gut level panic. He reached for her slightly rounded belly. She covered his hand with hers and shook her head.

"Of course you're not bothering me," he said. "Let me get my shoes and we'll go right now. Alex is at the hospital working with Sandy, so she's already there. Do you feel okay?"

Gena carefully walked inside and sat at the kitchen table. Her movements were stiff and awkward.

"I feel like I'm having cramps. Like they're about to get worse. My back is killing me." She held her breath, then let it out in a rush. "I'm losing the baby."

Etan tried to do the math, to remember what he'd read about miscarriages, but his brain refused to cooperate.

"Hold on, we don't know what's happening yet. We're too far along for that, aren't we? You were fine at your last checkup."

He stepped into his shoes and helped her stand. Her hand was now hot and trembling.

"I know, it's usually fine after five months, but the baby hasn't moved all day long. I don't think… I can't remember for sure, but I haven't felt anything for maybe a couple of days."

"Sandy will know better than both of us," Etan said, closing the door behind them. "Definitely better than me. Can you manage the stairs? We can use Alex's elevator, or I can go get Sandy."

"No, I can walk. I just didn't want to be alone."

Gena's breath caught, and she covered her face with both hands. Etan put his arms around her, desperately trying not to press on her belly. She squeezed him tight, sobbing against his chest. Her face was burning hot through his shirt.

"I thought I was doing everything right. Eating right, resting, I've never taken better care of myself in my whole *life*."

"You *are* doing everything right, Gena. Listen, we don't even know what's going on yet. I'm right here with you."

She made it down the four flights of stairs, but she grabbed his hand before they'd taken two steps down Main Street. No one was out in the cool, early afternoon. Probably at the high school or at the big garden, still unaware of this private, painful drama.

Her grip was strong enough to make his knuckles ache.

"I'm sure that's a contraction," she whispered, then gasped. "I'm so sorry."

Etan put his arm around Gena's waist, supporting as much of her weight as he could.

"Hang on, maybe not. Will you be okay here if I go get Sandy?"

She squeezed her eyes closed, shaking her head. After a few deep breaths, she looked up at Etan. Her brown eyes were rimmed with red.

"We should get to the hospital just in case Sandy can do something, but I think it's too late. My water just broke."

After the third time she had to stop and breathe through the waves of pain, Etan knew. His mind tried to convince him otherwise, but his heart had no doubts.

They were losing one of their babies, saying goodbye to a child before it was ever born.

Before *any* of their children were born.

And neither he nor Iris had seen this coming.

Chapter 9

THE DELIVERY ROOM at the hospital in Wolf Branch felt too quiet, too still, for such a joyful occasion. One mother-to-be paced the floor, each of the fathers and her own partner taking turns walking with her, holding her hand, rubbing her back.

Her partner - a woman who wouldn't be having her own baby today - did everything she could to stay happy and cheerful and honestly excited, but Alex caught Gena's unguarded expression more than he wanted to.

Thankfully the room wasn't the same cold, bright operating room where they'd lost the baby and left that part of their dream behind a few months before. This could have been a living room if you ignored the especially fancy adjustable bed with monitors built in.

Warm and comforting gold walls, soft rugs on the floor. Couches and chairs for all the hovering in-laws rather than a distant waiting room with uncomfortable plastic backside torture devices. And more than enough space for Alex, Etan, and Gena to fret and worry, wishing they could do more to help Iris.

Etan's mother Laura was proud to tell everyone how Anne and Evan – her own former in-laws and Etan's grandparents – had gotten this homelike birthing room set up. When they'd moved to Wolf

Branch decades ago, such things were unheard of in small town hospitals.

Sandy and her nurse Jeff checked in from time to time, but both of them said the same thing so far. Nothing they could do with labor progressing so well. They didn't expect to do much at all, really, besides calm folks down and stand by just in case.

Alex knew those words and the reassuring smiles rang hollow to everyone else as much as they did to him.

Yes, of course everything was fine.

Just like it had been for Gena's baby.

Until it wasn't.

And thinking that way would only make a wonderful thing sad and a bad thing worse.

He took his turn walking with Iris, leaving Etan and Gena to concentrate on the soon-to-be grandparents. They'd all agreed earlier that the flood of advice, even when offered with love and the best of intentions, was best channeled away from the laboring woman.

"Did you paint anything about today?" he said, taking her hand in his. It felt cool and small, but her grip was fierce. "Besides the one about family."

"They've all been jagged and strange lately. Like this baby dancing on my spine at the moment. She could have at least worn ballet slippers instead of stiletto heels."

"She, huh. Is that you or Sandy talking?"

Iris laughed, but it ended in a groan.

"Gena absolutely forbade Sandy from telling us one way or the other. She doesn't want me to tell her either. I've seen this little one's face in my dreams for weeks now. I hope I haven't let it slip before I wake up."

"Etan's been seeing a girl in his dreams, too," Alex said, smiling. "He threatened my life if I told him, so it's our secret for a little while longer."

They made another circuit of the big room, with Iris leaning against Alex twice to stretch her back. Neither of them said it, but Alex knew they were thinking of the little boy Gena had been carrying.

Sandy made it clear none of them had done anything wrong, and there was no reason they shouldn't try again. None of the four of them wanted to, not for a while.

"I'm sorry to ask this now," Alex said when they were on the far side from everyone else, "but are you sure you want us to raise this one? We're more than happy to, but not if it makes anything worse for you or Gena."

Iris shook her head, then pushed her black hair back over her ear.

"I think Gena's right. Us raising this one alone would be harder on her. Seeing her every day, thinking about what could have been. This way you two can focus on the baby, and I'll focus more on Gena. We'll see you plenty for nursing anyway."

"Fair enough. And I can't *thank* you enough."

"She's a lucky girl, getting to grow up with you." She stopped, hands on her knees while Alex rubbed her lower back. "I don't want to walk anymore. I think I'm ready. Walk me back to the bed and go get Sandy?"

Alex looked up and caught Etan's gaze. At his nod, Etan smiled and walked out.

The second Iris sat on the bed that had been lowered to make movement easier for her, Sandy, Jeff, Gena, and Etan seemed to materialize beside Alex.

His focus, his awareness and ability to know what was going on around him had shifted.

Narrowed and changed to a tunnel-like vision.

He knew everyone else was still there, including Etan's mother and Gena's parents. But the pattern recognition engine inside his head only saw, only understood one connection right now.

The tiny strand of light and life between him and the little girl who was about to enter their world.

His eyes saw Sandy adjust a monitor of some kind, attaching a cable to a transparent patch on Iris's hip. His ears heard low conversation between the two of them, but not a word registered with his brain. Sandy nodded and tapped again, and Iris's vise-like grip on Alex's hand eased.

His skin felt the cool air in the room. He tasted the tea they'll all shared earlier, the sweet, herbal blend Sandy swore would help all of them relax. Excitement mixed liberally with fear had Alex about as far from relaxed as he'd ever been in his life.

And still, the experience of his physical body felt muted, distant compared to the way this little girl would surely be transforming his heart.

He did mange to look into Etan's eyes, calling back all the conversations and hopes and dreams they'd shared about this moment. Always assuming they'd be in a Chicago hospital, with the great, teeming city waiting to welcome their children into a world that no longer existed.

The world that would greet this child might be utterly changed and empty, but she couldn't come into a room more full of love.

"Okay, Dads," Sandy said, looking up from her perch between Iris's thighs. "Everything is about to change. Better get ready."

She'd raised and adjusted the end of the bed into a nearly upright position, with Iris sitting against it and staring into Gena's eyes while she counted. Etan and Alex stood on either side, ready to brace Iris when she was ready to push.

Etan winked at Alex, clearly aware of his shell-shocked state. He mouthed *Ready?*

Alex shook his head and reached for his husband's hand. They leaned forward when Iris did, shoulders behind hers like Sandy had shown them. He felt her muscles tense, heat rolling off her flesh. Gena gripped Iris's hands, sitting on the bed beside her, never looking away from her face.

Alex couldn't have said when it was all over whether the delivery took ten minutes or ten hours. All he knew was the growing pull of that new life force, their daughter charging into the world, demanding every bit of attention from his mind and his heart.

Sandy handed the screaming bundle to Gena, who kissed the tiny, red, wrinkled forehead before turning to Iris's waiting arms.

Alex knew before he looked that the little girl had a thick fuzz of red hair.

Several of their endless discussions had been about names, and having to come up with names for a boy or girl had only made it harder. But Alex was thankful a thousand times over for all that talk now.

When Iris turned to him, smiling with tears in her eyes, he knew exactly what to do and what to say. He took the delicate creature with the healthiest lungs in all the world into his arms, only then noticing Etan stood beside him.

Alex put his free arm around his husband and kissed his cheek.

"Welcome to the world, Caela."

Chapter 10

Alex sat across from Gena in her apartment, watching her nurse their newest baby. She and Iris had both made it clear when Caela was born three years ago that they preferred him and Etan to just be honest about it instead of pretending not to look, then sneaking glances. Neither of them saw any reason on earth why they shouldn't watch such a lovely thing as feeding their babies.

Alex and Etan couldn't possibly have agreed more.

Gena held Connor to her left breast, eyes closed, rocking slightly. The sun caught her blonde hair as she shifted. Their tiny boy, only five weeks old, had understood from his first moments of life exactly what he was supposed to do. He latched onto her dark red nipple and stayed there whenever he had the chance.

"Do you ever resent it?" Alex said. "Having to do this over and over again?"

"You mean being pregnant? Or nursing?"

"Either one. They do go together."

"They do. This wasn't exactly what I planned, you know? When I worked my ass off for a law degree." She shifted, adjusting Connor along with her legs. "But everything changed all around us. If we don't do this, *especially* us, we'll all be gone in less than fifty years."

"That's almost exactly what I told Etan a long time ago," Alex said, smiling. "I hope you know how much we appreciate both of you."

"I know. You too, hon." She touched Connor's face and her breast, pulling her nipple away until he let go with a pop. "Plenty on the other side, hungry boy. Hey, have you had a chance to read through Iris's journal? The one from a year ago?"

"Not yet, but I did look at Etan's from two years ago. I think you're right about the dreams matching up now," he said, shifting his hips lower on the chair and crossing his legs. "I'm sorry I didn't look those over yet. We need to find a better way to manage things like this. We're spinning our wheels. Just because we don't have databases in our pockets anymore doesn't mean we have to be so disorganized."

"Well, maybe we need to talk about that," Gena said. Connor settled again, just as enthusiastically. "The Witnesses, all of us. You and I keep similar records, so we can cross-reference when we need to. We have no idea what everyone else is doing. We have to remember someone may be reading these long after we're not around to explain what we *meant* to say."

"Witness each other, you mean."

"That would be a nice change of pace, wouldn't it?" Gena said with a wicked smile. "Being the center of attention, at least among ourselves."

"I do sometimes feel like the town crier, repeat what I've heard and shut up. Especially since I can hardly ever get Etan to speak up in the Council. If we can at least get our records standardized somehow, have an idea what everybody is concentrating on, we'll have a much easier time verifying the dreams."

"Leave it to a lawyer and an engineer to recreate standards and practices," Gena said. "Some things never change, even after the end of the world. Let me interject a bit of *best* practices, then. We'd have to do this without the Dreamers."

"Otherwise we'll never know if the dreams come from them or from someone else. They shouldn't even read each other's journals, really. Listen, Gena, have you ever heard something bad enough in one of Iris's dreams that you didn't tell her or anyone else?"

She pursed her lips and looked away from him.

"Yeah. I kept what I saw in her paintings to myself in the beginning, a couple of times. Again before I had the miscarriage, before Caela was born. I knew something was wrong, but I pretended I didn't, even to myself. I thought if I admitted it, I'd let it come true. It did anyway. A few other times back in the world, too."

Alex nodded, but he couldn't speak. Not about the loss of their first child, or Etan's dreams about his father dying. He'd still never spoken to another person besides his husband about his father-in-law's sacrifice, and he didn't plan to. If anything so awful came up in the future, he'd love to at least have the option.

"Same here," he finally said. "It would be great to have someone else to talk to. Someone to just listen to some of this who didn't dream it."

"We can make sure these little ones get trained properly, too, so maybe they won't be bumbling along with no idea what they're doing. Like we are. He's just about finished."

Connor was finally getting full and sleepy. His mouth moved more slowly against Gena's nipple with every passing minute. Alex draped a thick towel over his shoulder and stood.

This was one of the many reasons he'd volunteered to bring their babies down while they were nursing so often. The scents, the warmth of their bodies. The heady sensation of holding such a tiny creature safe in his arms. All the rituals of feeding delighted him.

The babies might seem defenseless, but Alex never doubted he was the one disarmed.

"We'll have to do some of the training at home," Gena said. She lifted a drowsy Connor into Alex's arms. "They'll be up in the middle of the night like their parents are."

Alex breathed in their son's sweet milk breath before shifting Connor to his shoulder. He gently patted and rubbed his back, walking back and forth on the dark, flowery rug.

"I can't imagine trying to keep up with a bunch of them all at once," he said. "We won't know if they'll be Dreamers or Witnesses, or neither, until it starts. Maybe we can give them the basics, teach them the routines when they're younger. At least let them know what to expect whichever way it goes for them."

Gena walked quietly into the kitchen, returning with a huge glass of water, an apple, and a wedge of cheese.

"I never stop eating at this stage. Don't let me forget to give you the bottles for overnight. I'd be willing to bet the Council will want to keep focusing on work training for now, at least for the kids born before. The general consensus is we need farmers more than we need Dreamers."

"We'll have to have both," Alex said. He smiled when Connor's chest rumbled. "Etan's at the cannery right now."

"This is going to sound awful, but we have to train the ones who won't be on the Council or Dreamers or Witnesses just as carefully. We need them to all be on the same side."

"*Our* side." Alex glanced out the window toward the cannery, as if his husband would be able to hear him. He sat beside Gena, half caught up in the milk-drunk sleepiness and warmth radiating from the baby. "We'll have to merge the government and the religion together, much as Etan despises the idea. Otherwise we won't make it. Do you miss this part? With the ones Etan and I raise?"

She rubbed Connor's back, then touched his wispy brown hair.

"Sure, a little. It helps to have our own running around. I know they couldn't be in better hands than with you two. Honestly, I'm glad Iris has ours at her parents' place right now, and every time Etan's mom stays with them or keeps them. The quiet time does me a world of good. It's more exhausting than you can imagine nursing and being up with the babies or with Iris all night, too."

"Being up with Etan was exhausting enough." Alex kissed Connor's warm forehead. "Add these precious little screamers in and I don't *want* to imagine how tired you two get."

"You know we're more than halfway to a religion already, Alex, or something close enough. We can set that in stone as Witnesses."

"And we can try to live with the consequences. For us and our children."

Chapter 11

Meetings in the conference room at the Wolf Branch Town Hall weren't the nightmare Etan had convinced himself they'd be years ago. But he never stopped wishing he were back in the cozy little break room next door with Alex and a few of their friends.

This room was several times as large, with room for four typical long conference tables making a square. In theory, almost as egalitarian as a round table where they could all see each other, if not nearly as poetic. The current Council of fifteen fit easily, with room for at least twice that many in the future.

Etan didn't want to imagine that many sitting under the lights too bright for his taste, even with the usual slight dimming to save electricity. The old rectangular ceiling tiles full of tiny little holes made him feel like he was a kid at the dentist's office, bored and trying to count how many holes in each one.

The meeting's endless droning wasn't quite as bad as the whine of the dentist's drill, but some days he thought it came close. Once a month of these meetings was more than enough for him.

He had to admit the navy blue chairs were almost adjustable enough to lean that flat, with arms and lumbar support and headrests able to fit pretty much every variety of human. He kept meaning to ask his mother how the town had managed to pay for so many expensive chairs.

The pleasant, fruity aroma of their yaupon tea and Walt's honey covered the stuffiness of having the doors closed. Etan was thankful for the caffeine to keep himself awake, and a bit worried about how long everyone else would be able to keep talking.

Not entirely because of the tea half-finished in front of him, Etan's leg shook, an anxious movement he couldn't seem to control. He barely managed not to tap his heel against the flat gray carpet loud enough to disturb everyone else.

Even more than the usual routine meetings, nothing about this afternoon was going to be easy. Having the same awful dream several nights in a row convinced him he had to act, but the dread was only getting worse.

"It's going to be okay," Alex whispered.

He moved his hand along Etan's thigh, squeezing just above the knee until his nervous motion stopped.

"You're not alone, E," he said, only loud enough for Etan to hear. "I know the dream's been the same every night. I'm right here."

Etan managed a quick smile, and he covered Alex's hand with his own. The sense of responsibility was so strange, almost detached, but still deep within him.

He didn't remember this dream, not a shred of it. He'd read every word Alex had written down though. The words matched, almost perfectly night after night, on every precious sheet of paper.

And the words felt true.

The meeting washed over him even more slowly than usual, taking forever and going too fast at the same time. He surprised himself with how much he loved working at the cannery and teaching. But he was still bored with the day to day business of building their little group of survivors.

He knew it was crucial work, the only thing giving even a small number of humans a chance. But Etan could never quite manage to pay attention until it was his turn to speak.

He hadn't quite worked out how people having the same dreams could argue so much.

For once, he wished this dull part would just go on for the rest of the day, for the rest of all the days.

All too soon, George Light stood, his huge, dark brown hands held out as if in prayer.

"Let us now turn to the Dreamers."

Etan looked up, squeezing Alex's hand. George had used his own dreams to build a following before everything had gone to hell, a large and powerful church if his stories were to be believed. As much as that idea bothered Etan, George had brought many of those followers though to safety.

He'd also proven invaluable in helping the Council move forward. He knew how to turn prediction into prophecy, and leaders into prophets.

"Have any of you a Dream to share with us?" George said.

His former life as a preacher was on full display in his booming voice, capital letters clear enough to hear, and grand gestures taking in everyone in the room.

Etan held his breath, hoping someone, anyone would speak first. This Dream was too important to ignore, and he would have given his right hand to avoid having to do just that.

Iris looked at him then. She sat pushed back from the table, hands on her hugely swollen belly. Her pregnancy was going as well as her others had, with Gena beside her every bit as glowing and healthy at the same stage.

Right now though, Iris looked anything but maternal. She probably hadn't had this Dream yet, but she knew *he* had.

If Etan didn't speak, she was going to speak for him, and not kindly.

"I have… I've had a Dream I need to share," Etan said, then he turned to Alex. "We need to share."

"Please share with us, brothers," George said as he sat down.

Etan didn't dare try to stand on his shaking legs, but he did raise his voice. He'd never equal George, and he didn't bother trying.

He simply didn't want to have to repeat himself.

"We're going to have to start turning people away," he said, then he shook his head. "Not *away*, exactly, but we can't have unlimited people living here. We're going to need other settlements."

Etan's breath caught, and the whole long conversation opened up in his mind. He knew who was going to speak, who was going to argue, who was going to support him.

He didn't have these pre-memories as often as some of the others did, not nearly as much as Iris. Nowhere hear as much as his grandmother Anne had. This one was exceptionally clear. Seeing it didn't make going through it seem any easier.

He heard a deep sigh to his left, just as he expected.

"Don't you think that's a little premature, son?" Harry Mullins said. "There are barely a thousand of us here now. This town had almost five thousand with no problems, more during boom times."

Before Etan could speak, Alex was shaking his head. Alex was suspicious of Harry as much as Etan was of George. Harry's use of his own Dreams to make obscene sums of money might be unquestioned evidence of leadership ability in some circles, and that had been true in the past.

That was not true in this room filled with Dreamers and Witnesses.

Much of Harry's money had gone toward getting Wolf Branch ready. Buying up solar panels, wind turbines, and water turbines before the prices soared and supplies dried up at the end. Almost all the equipment Alex had installed and taught everyone how to maintain.

Still, Alex had his doubts.

And Alex had always especially hated being called *son* by anyone besides his own father, and Etan's.

"There were that many here, Harry, certainly," Alex said. "But there was also grid electricity, sewage treatment, modern medicine, grocery stores. We can't build back up to the same levels we had then, not all in one place."

"I believe you're underestimating what we can accomplish," Harry said, nodding to himself. "We've done very well for ourselves in such a short time, and that's only going to continue."

"Harry, you're forgetting we've called the Dreamers to speak," Iris said, her voice not inviting argument. "We don't even know what this was about yet. Please, Alex, tell us of the Dream."

Etan caught Iris' wink, and he smiled in return. He'd known she would speak, and he was no less grateful when she did. Alex held up his current journal, this one a thick spiral-bound notebook with a blue vinyl cover.

"The Dream was the same six nights in a row, with no variation. We have choices here, but they come with consequences. If we continue to let everyone who shows up settle here, we'll run out of resources. We won't have the food long before we run out of shelter. And worst of all, we won't be able to handle the waste. Disease will take hold, and we won't get through it this time."

He stopped, looking around the room. Etan was sure he wasn't the only one who noticed Alex looked at everyone but Harry Mullins. Harry crossed his arms, obviously wanting to speak but not willing to tangle with Iris, eight months pregnant or not.

"If we start now, we'll be ready before we have to deal with turning people away," Alex went on. "What we do now is crucial."

Etan tried to force himself not to look across the squared tables, even though he knew Mary Shadrin was going to speak. She was one of the few remaining Dreamers without a Witness, something he and others were starting to distrust.

She was also the source of most of the dissent in these meetings and in the community, as she had been from the beginning. She stood, her slender frame and delicate features vibrating with indignation.

Or at least that's what Etan let himself imagine to keep himself calm, knowing what she was going to say. Her gray-streaked hair and gaunt face too nearly matched the first vision he'd seen of her so many years ago.

"What exactly are you suggesting?" Mary said, scowling at Etan and Alex. "We can either turn people away to die or we can outright kill them? We've already suffered one slaughter over keeping our bounty to ourselves at gunpoint. What was the point of all this if we're going to start making the same stupid mistakes?"

"Don't even start with that, Mary," Alex said, his overly calm voice a warning. He took a slow, deep breath, then let it out in a rush through his lips. "They were going to steal everything we had, not join together in some kind of big happy commune. You know as well as I do they would have used those explosives to kill a lot more of us if they'd had the chance. Any other choice we made ended up with *all* of us dead."

A few people murmured, and Etan couldn't tell if they were agreeing or not. This time, Gena spoke.

"Iris and I know the raiders from Maple Ridge were capable of far worse, Mary. They *planned* far worse. Until we understand what Etan's Dream actually was, what it will become, we can't know how to move forward. In the years we've been listening to his Dreams, have any of them not come to the rest of us in time?"

The soft voices stopped, but Mary still stood. Neither Gena nor anyone else had to say Mary's Dreams rarely came to any of the rest of them. Whatever brought on the Dreams seemed to be erratic in her.

Mary tossed her long hair and straightened her shoulders.

"I have Dreamed of creating a security force, of turning people away," she said in a ringing voice. "And that was a nightmare. If we arm ourselves, if we create some kind of militia, we'll go down the very same road that got us here in the first place."

"Etan has not had that Dream yet, Ms. Shadrin," Alex said, his voice hard, but calmer. "But security may well be another choice we eventually face. You raise a crucial point. If we do nothing, if we don't protect what we've worked so hard for, we may be overrun like we would have been the day Connor Griffith died. That would *just* as surely end with many of us dead and humanity scattered into dust."

Alex stood, bringing everyone's attention to him and Etan. And away from Mary

"If we make sure to keep ourselves safe, that's the only thing that can prevent the violence. We're not saying we must slaughter every person who staggers into town, or even that we need armed guards just yet. All we were suggesting is we take new people in, make sure they're healthy, then get them ready to settle someplace else."

Etan closed his eyes, wishing this would come to an end. Mary was never going to agree, no matter what he or Alex said. Her suggestion of a security force sent a chill through him that he felt pass through many others in the room.

If they'd set up some kind of patrols before the final collapse years before, his father might still be alive.

They couldn't forget what Mary said, even when so many of her Dreams were broken.

But Mary was going to stand alone today. Everyone else might not be happy with turning survivors away, but they wouldn't be willing to ignore such a strong Dream.

Logic mattered less and less. Not as much as belief.

The religion had taken shape all around Etan. Even worse, largely *because* of him.

"So you choose to ignore my Dream of ruin?" Mary said, her voice breaking. "We'll just send them out into the wilderness and wish them luck?"

"We'll help them until enough are gathered to start a new community," Alex said. "And when they're ready, one of our families will go with them. People who've been part of rebuilding, who know what needs to be done and what to avoid. That's one reason we've been studying how to grow things we can't grow here. We have to find new ways to feed ourselves, and part of that is settling in other areas."

"Of course, of course," Harry Mullins said, not quite able to hide his smile. "Trade. We have to reestablish trade, get ourselves back on a paying basis."

"No, not like that," Etan said, surprised at the confident sound of his own voice. "We'll have surplus and so will they. The other communities will be able to find more supplies of medicine, eyeglasses, clothing, things we're going to run out of here. We'll have to learn to share the supplies in a fair way. And we will *not* be using food for leverage or for profit. We can't afford to do that."

Alex sat, then ducked his head toward Etan and grinned, keeping himself out of everyone else's sight. Etan rolled his eyes and smiled back.

Alex had been trying to get him to speak up more in meetings for years.

"Listen," Alex said, "just because we can see *what* needs to be done, what we have to do to survive, doesn't mean we see all the details of *how*. Etan said this Dream felt like an opening, like something all of us would participate in. Everyone may get a different part, and each part is going to make a difference. I don't like the idea of turning people away either, or Mary's Dream of arming ourselves. But if we don't take steps now, before it becomes a problem, we're not going to make it. We won't. Our children won't. Our grandchildren won't."

The room was silent for a long while, and even Mary finally sat. Iris looked around the room, then got slowly to her feet with Gena's support.

Etan knew no one missed the significance of Alex's words and the shape of Iris' body, and Gena's. They might have been the first such arrangement four years ago, but they were only one of many now.

Iris standing proudly before them, carrying Alex and Etan's baby, spoke louder than anyone's words possibly could.

"We've worked too long and too hard to let everything die out in a couple of generations," she said, looking at Etan and Alex in turn. "We've all had to adjust, and some things have been much harder than others. I believe this will be the next step we need to take. I believe this Dream is true."

At her words, the ceremonial invitation to accept or reject a Dream, the tension finally left Etan's body. None of this was going to be easy, but at least they were going to move forward.

Harry Mullins stood as Iris carefully sat down.

"I believe this Dream is true."

Even without his memory guiding him, Etan knew no one was going to move to validate Mary's Dream.

Hardly anyone did anymore.

One after another, the people around the table stood and spoke, adding support to what they all had to do together. Dreamers and

Witnesses, often paired as couples but some as companions, raised their voices and judged Etan's Dream true.

Finally only Mary Shadrin and George Light were left.

Mary looked around the room, meeting everyone's gaze. She looked into Etan's eyes last, and he knew no words or gesture would change her mind. She shook her head and looked down at her hands.

Etan had seen it coming, but some part of him was surprised, and hurt. She wasn't saying this wasn't a good idea, that they shouldn't take this action.

She was denying the truth of what he'd seen. That denial was far more serious than an opposing vote.

Etan knew it seemed to call his Dreams into question, his Dreams or Alex's ability to remember them. The lowered eyes all around the table and his own churning gut told him Mary had called her own ability to be part of this Council into doubt.

Her judgment could no longer be trusted, any more than her own Dreams could.

George compressed his lips, but he got to his feet, going last as was his tradition.

"I also believe this Dream is true, and I *declare* that it is so," he said, his voice filling the room and somehow filling their bodies. "Dreamers and Witnesses, all of us must be watchful for the parts we will all play. Let us all go forward together, today and well into the future."

PART III

A REMNANT OF THE OLD WORLD

Chapter 12

Tiny hands grasping along Etan's back and ribs, trying their best to tickle, dragged him from a dead sleep. He wanted nothing more than to ignore the giggling efforts to wake him after the night he'd passed. A particularly rough pinch jerked him into awareness.

"Over to this side of the bed, hellions," Alex said, trying to keep his voice low. "Daddy E isn't ready to wake up yet."

"Why not?" Gwen said, her high voice much louder. "*We* gotta be up!"

"Cause he works all night long while you lazy sods lay in bed and snooze. Over here or you can't go with me today."

Etan opened his eyes and stretched just as Gwen and Connor thundered around to Alex. The bedroom was still dark, a sliver of early dawn pink visible through the window. He was constantly amazed at how much noise four-year-old and three-year-old feet could make.

"Daddy E don't sleep?" Gwen said.

"*Doesn't.*" The bed shifted as Alex sat up. "Daddy E doesn't sleep much lately."

"I don't sleep at all with you two rumbling around here." Etan turned to see both kids staring at him with comical surprise in the faint light, Gwen's blonde head several inches taller than Connor's brown curls.

"Morning Daddy E!" Connor cried, running right back around to Etan.

"Daddy A said you don't sleep," Gwen said. She stood with her hands on her hips, clearly disapproving of her little brother's giggles when Etan picked him up.

"Sometimes I do, sweetheart. I just didn't last night. Where are you all off to so early?"

"Well, it's not that early," Alex said with a half smile. "Not by farmer standards, anyway. Linda asked me to help out today, with a bunch of teenagers ready to learn how to harvest soybeans. I might take these two pests with me, put them to work."

"Wanna work!" Connor shrieked into Etan's face. Alex picked him up, slung low under one arm like a sack, then lifted Gwen to his other hip.

"You *will* work, especially if you keep squalling like that." Alex looked at Etan and frowned. "I think Daddy E needs to stay right here and get more sleep, don't you?"

"I'll be fine, just let me get some tea. Linda asked me to help, too."

"Forget it, young man," Alex said. "We'll be fine. Seriously, get some rest. You're exhausted."

Etan couldn't manage to argue. He'd spent a terrible night in and out of Dreams, never quite waking up enough to understand what was going on around him.

The same thing had been happening for the last few weeks, but Alex couldn't make sense of what the Dreams were about either.

Sometimes they were just static.

Etan had just about fallen back asleep when a warm body snuggled up against his chest, another against his back. Alex kissed his cheek, then whispered close to his ear.

"These two will be out for another couple of hours. Caela's off with me. Sleep if you can. Maybe you can meet us for lunch."

Etan nodded without opening his eyes. More stomping moved

through the apartment, Alex's deep voice mixed with their children's higher tones. Finally all he heard was Eddie and Meghan's regular breathing.

He joined them before three more of his own breaths.

The Dream shattered their lives barely an hour later.

Chapter 13

Linda was already out in the soybean fields beyond the cannery when Alex got there, her grey head standing out among all the teenagers around her. None of the kids had clear memories of football or baseball fields instead of neat rows of fading green plants stretching nearly out to the mountains surrounding them.

Caela, Gwen, and Connor ran to the group of older kids, each sending wisps of steam into the mid-October air with their chatter. The light and the last few days let Alex know it would be warm enough for the short sleeves they all wore under their jackets by the afternoon.

"Where do you need us?" Alex said as he joined Linda and several of her former students.

"Help me keep an eye on these troublemakers," she said, slapping Jimmy Adams on the back. He'd been one of Alex's and Etan's most challenging, and most talented, students right before everything fell apart. In his twenties now, Jimmy stood nearly as tall as Alex. "They're going to keep the new ones in line so us old folks don't have to."

"Mr. Griffith, Etan I mean, just threatened to throw me in one of those giant pots if I got too far out of line," Jimmy said with a grin. "I figure that's all there is to it."

"More or less," Alex said. "I'll keep the little ones out of your way."

"No, they're right where they need to be." Linda shielded her eyes with one hand, watching the kids playing with the rangy red hound dogs. "I've been thinking about ways we could get children involved since we finally have a bunch of them again."

"You mean with farming?" Alex said. He watched Jimmy, another young man, and two young women getting the teenagers organized. His children listened to every word they said with wide eyes. "Connor was shouting his fool head off this morning about wanting to *work*."

"That's what I had in mind," Linda said. "Pollination isn't a game for people my age."

"We could make it into a game for them," Alex said. "Anne saw it years ago, the little ones doing the hand pollination. It's as good a way to help them start learning as any."

"They *are* a lot lower to the ground," Linda said.

The teenagers spread out into the rows, recycled cloth bags slung over their shoulders. The plants closest to them were in full sunlight, so they worked from there toward the still-dark section close to the mountainside.

Caela, Gwen, and Connor had small bags of their own hanging past their knees. The dogs ambled from one person to the next, tails high and wagging, sniffing for treats.

"Where's Etan this morning?" Linda said.

"He hasn't been sleeping well," Alex said. "Worse than usual. He did want to help, but I told him to get some more rest."

"We'll do fine. Dreaming all night has to keep him exhausted."

One of the dogs lowered her head to the ground, her tail wagging faster. She darted forward, turning left, then right.

"He normally…" Alex trailed off, distracted by the abrupt change in the dog's motion. He shook his head, trying to keep his words straight. "This doesn't seem like a Dream, not a real one. Nothing I can follow, anyway."

Several of the other dogs joined the first one, all of them with their noses down.

The pattern took shape between one beat of Alex's heart and the next.

"Anything different out in that old equipment shed?" he said without looking away from the dogs. "They seem to be headed that way."

"Don't think so." Linda shaded her eyes again, the corners of her mouth turned down. "We hardly ever keep anything but tools in there. It was great for sports equipment, too drafty for food."

Alex took a few steps forward, his eyes on the small building still hidden in deep shadow. The rows, the motion of the hounds, even his children's breath rising into the air pointed toward that shed he and Etan had cleaned out together years ago.

The first dog to catch the scent raised her nose, her bay shocking in the quiet morning air. When she ran toward the thick trees beyond the fields, the others joined in her musical and somehow unsettling chorus.

Alex had seen the hunters training these dogs, heard them out in the woods on the trail of deer or elk. The barking was faster now, too quick to count, and far more furious than when they were chasing game.

"They're onto something," Alex said. For the first time since not long after Etan's father died, he wished he had his gun at his hip. "I'll be right back."

The dogs resumed their zigzag search, moving from the woods to surround the shed. Alex glanced toward the group of children, making sure his three were still occupied. A few of the older ones were watching, and Jimmy Adams was walking toward the shadows himself.

Alex started to wave him back, then reconsidered.

If the dogs *had* scented something, he might not want to face it alone.

Chapter 14

Etan woke, eyes wide, heart pounding, Meghan's sleepy protests in his ears.

"Too tight, Addy E. Too tight."

He forced his arms to relax even though his entire body was screaming for movement, for action.

Gods, how could they have been so stupid?

"I'm sorry, Meghan, but we have to get up. Right now. Eddie, wake up. I need to go find Daddy A."

Etan put Meghan on her feet then got to his own, shaking his head. He didn't have time for tea or anything else.

Alex didn't have time.

"Eddie, we can't go back to sleep now. We have to go."

The dark-haired boy, barely a year and a half old, gripped the covers and squeezed his eyes closed. Etan scooped him up blanket and all.

"Meghan, I need you to be a big girl right now. Can you do that? I need you to get dressed as fast as you can. Right now."

He forced himself to focus over the screams crashing through his mind.

Kids, teachers.

A snarling face he barely recognized as human but would remember for the rest of his days.

Alex's screams.

"Big girl shirt?" Meghan said, rubbing her eyes. "Caela's shirt?"

"Whatever you want, baby. We have to go."

Etan stepped into his shoes and followed into her room, untangling Eddie's fingers and dropping the blanket as he went. Meghan pulled her drawer open as he did the same on the other side of the room.

"Fast as you can," he said, pulling out pants he hoped were Eddie's size. "You can finish up at Mama G's place, okay?"

"Go to Mama G's?" Eddie said, his voice still soft with sleep.

"You both are. I have to go see Daddy A for grown up stuff, so you have to stay here."

"Go see Daddy A!" Meghan wailed.

No, he couldn't deal with this. Meghan stood with one of Caela's old shirts hanging down to her knees, her green eyes wide and full of tears.

"Now listen. We're not going to argue, understand me?" Etan hated the sharp tone in his voice, but he couldn't wait any longer. "You're staying downstairs with your brothers and sisters. Let's go, right now."

Meghan started crying when he picked her up. Rather than suffer hearing loss, Etan let her slip down into sack position the way Alex often carried them.

Alex.

"More blood," he whispered, tears welling in his own eyes. "He's not bleeding enough."

By the time he made it down the flight of stairs, both kids were howling. At least Gena and Iris would hear them coming.

Iris opened the door before he knocked.

"What's going on? Where's Alex? Neither one of us can see. Did you Dream?"

"Something at the fields," he said, handing Meghan to Iris, Eddie to Gena. Both women looked as terrified as he felt. "I'm sorry to-"

"Go, you're running out of time," Gena said, her voice tight. "He doesn't have long."

Etan moved as fast as he dared, taking three flights of stairs two at a time. As soon as he stepped out into the cool morning air, the Dream exploded back into his mind.

Someone in the woods, so thin and dirty he couldn't tell if it was a man or a woman. Hiding close by for so long, finally desperate enough to try stealing their food or tools or weapons.

The dogs, lean and rangy and coats nearly as red as Alex's beard. Noses to the ground, zigzagging across the field.

Tracking into the woods, then back to the storage shed. Swarming around it, noses high, throats baying.

Alex watching, then glancing at the crowd of kids scattered through the rows of beans. Caela and Gwen and Connor not far away, focused on the fuzzy green pods that fit so perfectly into their small hands.

Etan ran through the middle of town, screaming at everyone he saw to bring help.

Alex walking slowly around and into the shed. Never noticing Connor following with dramatic sneaking steps. The dogs running into the small building behind him, barking furiously at the open window on the far side.

Alex stepping back outside to see the scrawny creature grab the little boy.

Their son's scream bringing every head up and turning their way.

George Light stepped into the the doorway of the food pantry, Walt Colley beside him.

"Find Sandy!" Etan shouted. "Bring one of the rescue trucks out to the fields. Now!"

Gwen running toward her brother. Six-year-old Caela grabbing her little sister, screaming so hard she almost fell herself.

Alex holding both shaking hands up, walking forward. Calling the dogs back. Trying to reason with a person a decade past reason.

Connor nearly disappearing into filthy rags as the creature backed toward the woods.

Alex never saw the rusty knife.

Chapter 15

Alex tried to grab the dog closest to him. She twisted out of his grasp, her bark fast as a machine gun. His body was burning hot, freezing cold.

If the filthy thing ran off into the woods, they might never find Connor.

"No," he said, stepping forward. "Let him go. I'm not going to hurt you."

The bundle of filth and rags was small, barely past Alex's chest. It had more than enough strength to hold his shrieking child just out of his reach.

"Please don't hurt him. Can't you hear how scared he is?"

The dogs circled, nipping at the creature grasping Connor, howling and barking. Alex smelled the stench of long-unwashed human, his own stinking sweat. He held up shaking hands.

"Get back! I'll call them off if you let him go!"

The vaguely human shape took another step back. Fierce brown eyes, almost hidden in matted hair, watched Alex. Glanced at the shelter of the trees.

"We can help you," Alex said. "Just let my son go."

He saw the others out of the corner of his eye, moving closer. If they could just get between the creature and the woods, he might have a chance.

Caela and Gwen's cries cut through the noise, driving shards of glass into Alex's heart.

He would have sworn he heard Etan, shouting in the distance.

"I will *not* let you do this. Let him go!"

Alex moved and the thing stumbled and fell backward into the dust. Alex jumped forward into the middle of snarling dogs, grunting savage, and his screaming baby boy.

He grabbed at Connor's shirt, dragging him out of dirt-caked fingers and pushing him back. Trusting someone would catch his son, Alex closed his hands around the painfully thin throat.

His own throat was shouting, bellowing, but he could barely hear himself over the roaring inside his head.

Connor was safe.

No more compassion. No more mercy.

Alex held only fury in his hands and in his heart.

A shift, motion beneath him.

Etan's voice cutting through the howling in his mind.

A blow that passed through his whole body, deep and hard enough to take his breath.

The desperate need for air cooled Alex's fury in an instant.

Chapter 16

Etan's eyesight and his vision clashed, stuttered. Moving into real time.

Alex running out of time.

He heard people shouting behind him. The piercing shriek of his little boy was still impossibly far off.

The community garden he and Alex had labored over was full of autumn herbs and flowers, the scent heady in the rising heat. Around the bulk of the greenhouse Alex worked so hard to build.

Etan finally saw the class across the fields.

So far away. Yet he could hear his husband's shout as he took another step toward their son.

Every step brought Etan closer to too late.

"Alex, stop!"

Alex moved again, the dogs barking and circling. Only a few steps separated his body from the filthy, dull blade.

Linda grabbed up Caela and Gwen, shouting to the older kids to move back.

A hundred feet now. Fifty.

Alex stepped forward. The pathetic figure stumbled, falling backward with Connor still clutched to its chest. Alex darted forward, tangling with cries of inhuman fury and sobbing boy.

Twenty feet away.

Connor staggered out of the mess, through the howling dogs. One of the older boys snatched him up and ran toward the staring group. Another young man ran toward the bodies twisting in the dusty soil.

"The *knife*, Alex! The knife!"

Alex shifted on top of the thing, his fingers around its neck. He howled louder than the dogs, terrible in his fury.

Etan saw the reddish blade sink into his lover's body from ten feet away.

Alex's voice cut off. He twisted away and grabbed at his side.

Etan had no voice left for his own cry.

Etan and Jimmy Adams, his long-ago smart ass student, grabbed Alex's shoulders and dragged him away.

"Get down!" a man shouted from behind them.

A hail of fist-sized rocks struck the creature before it could stand. These same teenagers had piled them up, helping clear the field when they were toddlers.

All was still except for his husband's labored breathing. Etan gasped for his own breath, heart pounding in his ears, sweat running down his face and back.

"Alex," Etan said, falling to his knees, his voice a harsh whisper. "Don't move. Sandy will be right here."

"Where's Connor? The girls?"

"They're fine, now be *still*."

Alex's face was pale and tight, his mouth twisted. His chest hitched with his struggles to draw air into his body. Etan tried to lift his fingers away from his side.

"Get the kids away, Etan. Just need to catch my breath. Don't know what the hell that thing punched me with, but I'm okay."

"The kids *are* away, let me see."

Etan lifted Alex's hands and pulled up his shirt. A jagged wound at least three inches long stood out just under his ribs. Blood welled up to mark his pale skin, spilling down his side.

Not enough blood.

"See?" Alex tried to raise up, then groaned and coughed. "Hardly a scratch."

A moan built from low inside Etan's chest, near where Alex's life was spilling away in his own.

"Alex, listen to me. You're bleeding inside. You have to be still. I hear the truck coming now."

Shouts and footsteps approached with agonizing slowness. Etan wanted to see how close they were, but he was too terrified Alex would be gone when he looked back.

"Just help me stand up," Alex said, his voice weaker. "Don't waste fuel for a truck."

"Gods, *listen* to me, you stubborn jackass," Etan said. Tears dropped onto the dusty ground, onto Alex's skin. "Something is wrong inside. You have to let them help you."

"Let me see, Etan," Sandy said from right behind him.

"It stabbed him," Etan said, shifting out of the way but not letting go of Alex's hand. "He should be bleeding more. I Dreamed all the blood stayed inside."

"Hey, Alex," she said, kneeling beside Etan. "Your neck or head hurting? Anything numb?"

"Wish I was numb. Can't breathe right. Damn boulder...in my chest when I try."

"Okay. I'm going to feel your stomach now. I'm sorry, it might hurt."

She pressed in a line away from the wound, barely enough to move the flesh. Alex grimaced at first, then relaxed as she moved lower.

When she reached his abdomen, she shook her head.

"Hard as a rock," she said. "Probably got his spleen. How you feeling, Alex?"

"Like shit," he said, trying to smile. "Didn't hurt until just now. Don't think I can walk."

His hand was sweaty in Etan's despite the cool morning, his forehead clammy under Etan's lips.

Sandy shouted at the crowd milling around behind them.

"There's a stretcher in the truck! Bring it and enough people to lift him, now!"

"Someone get it?" Alex said. "Whatever attacked me?"

"Don't worry, sweetie," Etan said. He glanced at the bundle of rags on the ground, several men and women surrounding it. Harry Mullins walked toward them with a thick rope coiled over his shoulder. "I'll take care of that."

George Light grasped Etan's shoulder when he tried to climb into the bed of the huge farm truck with Alex.

"Hang on, you need to see to your children."

"Linda has them, George. I need to go with him."

"Etan, listen, listen to me," he said, his rich voice soothing Etan through his panic. "I know you're scared, but Alex is in the best hands he can be. He'll be all right for now. Don't you feel that?"

"He might not make it through the surgery! I can't let him go in there alone."

"George is right," Sandy said, taking Etan's hand. "We have him stable. The hospital is barely five minutes away. We'll send the truck right back for you. I promise."

"He's got to be terrified," Etan whispered, trying not to fall apart.

"I'm sure he is," George said, "but he knows Sandy will do her best for him." He put his arm around Etan and turned him back toward the field. "Your babies just saw one of their fathers get stabbed. Go see to them. He'd want you to."

Etan closed his eyes, gritting his teeth against the agonizing heat tearing through his chest. Alex got stabbed trying to protect Connor, and he would have done the same for any child.

He climbed up to the back of the truck where Alex lay on the stretcher. He was terribly pale, but he squeezed Etan's hand.

"The kids?" he said, confusion in his eyes. "Are they safe?"

"*You* kept them safe," Etan said. "I'll meet you at the hospital in a few minutes, okay? Sandy's going to take good care of you."

Alex squeezed his eyes closed when the truck started.

"Don't let them see me like this, E. Love you."

"I won't. I love you, Alex. Hang on. I'll be there as soon as I can."

Chapter 17

THE PAIN ARRIVED loud and clear when hands lifted Alex onto the stretcher. He knew they didn't mean to hurt him, not like that maniac who was trying to steal their little boy. But the shift and motion woke up a dark heat inside his chest. Trying to force air into his lungs had been hard enough before fire settled under his ribs.

His head swam when they lifted him, making the blue sky and Etan's green eyes fade to gray. Alex gritted his teeth, trying to stay in the world.

"Still with us, Alex?"

That was Sandy, at least he thought so. She sounded a thousand miles away, her words distorting with the impossibly fast beat of his heart.

"Not quite." His voice sounded tinny in his ears. "About to pass out."

"That's blood loss and shock," she said. "Hang in there if you can."

Alex couldn't focus on who was holding the stretcher, but he felt it when his back hit the bed of the truck a little too hard. He couldn't spare enough breath to cry out, even when pain forced a silent scream.

The pressure on his chest was worse than the buzzing in his ears.

The truck jounced on its springs, waking up the inferno in his ribs a little more.

Someone grabbed his hand.

Etan.

Alex would have given anything to be able to hear what his husband said, but the noise in his ears was too loud. Etan disappeared, and the truck lurched into motion.

Gray took over the world for several beats of his racing heart.

Chapter 18

The sky moved, shifting smoothly over Alex's head. He was having a terrible time focusing, but he could see the motion. He could feel it.

Was he in the back of a truck? That made no sense. People squeezed in around him, containers he couldn't see well enough to recognize lined the sides.

Something was wrong with him, something about his chest.

A fire burned deep inside of him.

A *fire*.

Connor was lost in a fire.

"Get him away from here," Alex said.

A woman leaned close to him, her fingertips on his throat just under his jaw.

"Get who away? We're almost there."

"Don't let Connor near this fucking truck!"

The shout, or as close as he could get to it, left Alex coughing, gasping for enough air to stay conscious through the flaring pain.

"Connor's with Etan, Alex," she said. "You protected him. We're going to do the same for you."

"He *won't* run. Full of bombs. Taking it right to him!"

"No, hon, no." She brushed his hair back, then touched his forehead. "We don't have any bombs. Not one. I promise. Your Connor is safe."

Alex shook his head, tears squeezing out of his eyes, hot against the cold sweat covering his shivering body. He caught glimpses of the red brick buildings behind her, foggy but unmistakable.

They were driving right through the middle of Wolf Branch in a truck full of explosives, every bit of it unstable.

Connor – Etan's father and the closest thing Alex ever had to one – was at the end of that road.

At the end of his life.

"Can't watch him die again. Get me away."

"Alex, this will all make sense once we get you stabilized." The woman's voice sounded full of tears. "That was years ago. Etan's father died saving all of us. I'm telling you your son is safe. Connor *is* safe, thanks to you."

Before he could catch enough breath to speak again, to beg this woman to warn Connor away before it was too late, Alex recognized the faded blue awning in front of the emergency room.

"We've got to lift you again," she said. "Stay with us if you can."

He couldn't.

Chapter 19

Etan climbed down and stood beside Walt Colley, watching the truck drive slowly away. He held up a hand to Sandy in the back, hoping she'd tell Alex.

He lowered his hand to his eyes, the terror and sorrow getting the best of him. Walt put strong arms around Etan, humming low and soft.

"We'll get you back to him," Walt said, leaning back and holding Etan's shoulders in his huge hands. "Let's get you to your babies first, then I'll take them home to their mammas."

Etan finally got a good look at Walt, the first thing that got through to his whirling mind besides Alex's blood where it wasn't supposed to be. Walt's eyes were red and wet, and he'd lost his constant green baseball cap somewhere. Wild gray hair stood up all over his head.

Etan had heard Alex talk countless times about how Walt welcomed him to Wolf Branch all those years ago. How Walt helped him feel at home when he needed it most.

Now Alex's good friend was trying to talk sense into Etan through his own worry and fear. Etan knew he'd left any kind of sense or calm behind when he'd left their apartment.

The least he could do was listen.

He let Walt walk with him over to where Linda sat on the ground, Connor curled up in her lap, Gwen tucked under her arm. Caela ran over to Etan, hitting so hard she knocked him back a couple of steps.

She was a perfect miniature version of Alex, from curly red hair to blue eyes now full of tears to sometimes furious temper. Etan knelt on one knee beside her.

"Is Daddy Alex going to die?" Caela said.

"Doctor Sandy is taking care of him."

"But that monster hurt him with a knife!"

Etan pulled her close, and her arms went around his neck squeezing tight. Her horrible sobs ripped Etan apart.

"I know. He got Connor away from the monster. Doctor Sandy will do the same for him. I'm so sorry you saw that, baby."

"I wish it never, ever happened," she said. Her voice trembled, and she hiccuped trying to catch her breath. "I don't want it to happen anymore."

"I wish it never happened too. Sweetheart, can you help Walt and Linda with the little ones? I know you're upset, but they could use someone to keep the babies calm. Can you do that?"

"Where are you going, Daddy?" She sat on his knee, gripping his arm so tight it hurt. "I'm scared."

"I'm going to help with Daddy Alex, that's all. I'll be home to you as soon as I can. You can stay with Iris and Gena. They'll make sure you're not scared."

"Is Daddy Alex scared?"

Etan squeezed his eyes closed, trying to turn his head so their daughter wouldn't see him cry. She caught his face with both hands, not even big enough to cover his cheeks. He opened his eyes.

Caela stared at him. She didn't say a word, but his heart knew she was begging him to tell her the truth.

"Yes, hon. He's scared."

She nodded, her features solemn.

"Tell him not to be. Tell him to come home where it's safe, as soon as he can."

Etan nodded, unable to speak. He was relieved when Caela

turned to take Walt's big rawboned hand. And just as relieved when Walt held out the other to help him get to his feet.

By the time he reached Linda, Gwen and Connor were staring at him. Connor was dirty and had his thumb firmly in his mouth, but he looked unhurt.

They both held out their arms to Etan. He didn't try to hide his relief this time.

"Are they okay?" he said, standing with four little arms wrapped tight around his neck.

"They're upset, but I don't think they're hurt," Linda said. Her gray hair had mostly escaped its bun, and she was streaked with dust and sweat.

"Are you?"

"Pretty shook up," she said, tears cutting fresh tracks through the dirt on her face. "I'm so *sorry*, Etan. It happened so fast, I couldn't get them away. I should have been watching Connor."

"No, Linda, no. Connor's going to be all right. And if…" Etan breathed deep a couple of times before he could go on. "If one of the kids had gone in there instead, it would have been worse."

"Still, I'm sorry. Do you need me to take them home?"

"Walt is going to, but he may need help if you want."

"Where's Daddy A?" Gwen said, her face pressed against Etan's ear.

"He had to go see Doctor Sandy. She's going to make him all better."

"Bad thing," Connor whispered around his thumb. "Bad thing hurt Daddy A."

"Yeah, that was a bad thing, baby," Etan said. He glanced toward town, where he'd seen Harry and the others dragging the heavily bound figure. "The bad thing is gone. Can't hurt you or Gwen or me or Daddy A anymore. Never, ever."

Etan heart sped up at the rumble of the truck, the rare sound of an engine unmistakable in the silence, just as it crested the hill by the cannery.

Was it already too late?

Walt saw Etan's face and stepped to his side, Caela still holding his hand.

"I still feel like he's doing okay," he said, nodding. "Sandy did too, remember? You best get to him, though."

"Listen, Gwen, Connor," Etan said. "I have to go help Daddy A. Mama Gena and Mama Iris are going to take care of you for a little while."

They both moaned, saying no over and over again in his ears. Etan squeezed them tight.

"I'm so sorry. I have to go. I'll be there as soon as I can. I'm sorry."

Their moans escalated when Walt and Linda pulled them away. Etan separated their fingers as gently as he could, kissing their tiny hands.

"I'll be home as soon as I can," he said. "We both will."

Gwen and Connor both cried and reached out for him as Walt and Linda walked away. Caela held both of the adult's hands, but she kept looking back over her shoulder.

Etan was thankful the truck stopped right beside him. Every bit of strength and courage had been wrung out of him.

He had a terrible feeling he was going to need more than he'd ever had.

He and his family weren't even half an hour into a long, long nightmare.

Chapter 20

Icy wetness slipped over Alex's chest and stomach, dragging him back to some pale imitation of consciousness. A sharp scent burned his nose, and the pressure still weighed on his chest.

He felt painfully bright lights against his face before he managed to open his eyes. Huge round spotlights hung above him. He narrowed his eyes against the brightest glare he'd seen in years.

Had lights always been so harsh in the old world?

The wetness withdrew, but an irritating, ticklish buzzing replaced the chill. He flinched away, then groaned at the tearing sensation in his ribs.

"Hey Alex," a deep voice said. Not Etan. "Jeff here, Sandy's nurse. Try to hold still. I don't want this to hurt."

"What to hurt? What the hell are you doing?"

"I just finished cleaning up the blood so I can see a little bit better. Now I'm going to get the hair off where we need to work. You're feeling the clippers."

Alex tried to raise up from the table enough to see his chest, but the pain only dug deeper. The man wearing purple scrubs and matching hat touched his shoulder. Alex realized his own worn out blue work shirt was gone.

"No, don't try to move like that," Sandy said. She appeared

beside Jeff, dressed in a matching shirt and hat. "Feel a little bit better?"

"A little. Not so damn cold, at least. What did you do?"

"We haven't done anything yet besides give you a couple of units of blood and fluids." Sandy leaned down to look at whatever Jeff was doing, then moved back. "We needed to get you stable before surgery."

"Surgery," he said, trying to force his groggy brain to work. "I don't understand."

"Do you remember the shed out in the fields, Alex?" Sandy said. "The person trying to get Connor?"

He smelled filthy human flesh, heard their little boy screaming.

"Etan was right," he said. "It stabbed me."

"Yeah, got you pretty good. Your spleen is bleeding, so we'll have to take at least part of that. We're going to get a look and do our best to repair whatever we find."

"You're taking out my spleen? I don't even know what that means, Sandy. Don't I need it?"

She nodded at Jeff, then leaned closer to Alex.

"It means if we don't get in there quick, you'll bleed to death, hon. We'll save part of your spleen if we can, but you'll be fine. We'll have to watch you for infections, and you will have to take it easy."

"Is that why I can't breathe? My spleen?"

Sandy pursed her lips, watching Alex for several seconds before she answered.

"I hope that's your diaphragm. The muscle that helps move your lungs."

"But it might not be."

She tilted her head to the side and shook her head.

"We don't know yet. Don't worry until we see what's going on."

Alex wished he could sit up and look her in the eye. He settled for the scowl Etan knew so well.

"Come on, Sandy. You know me better than that. You can't exactly wake me up in the middle to discuss what's going on. Just *tell* me."

"You're right," she said with a shrug. "Your lung isn't collapsed, at least not that I can tell without an x-ray. I don't want to take that long since I have to go in anyway. We're pushing it right now. I'll just say it's a hell of a lot easier to repair your diaphragm if it didn't nick your lung."

Alex closed his eyes, turning his face away from the bright lights.

"Am I going to wake up?"

He didn't say what he was thinking.

Will I leave all of them alone and lonely?

Will I ever see my children, or sleep beside my husband again?

"Look at me, Alex." When he did, her eyes were bright. "You want me to be honest, so I will. This is a serious injury. Assuming we get your spleen in time, we'll still have to do our best to clean the wound out and put you back together. *Nothing* about this is going to be easy. I'm going to do everything I can to get you home to your family. Understand?"

"So will I and everyone else," Jeff said. "I think most of the town is in the waiting room donating blood."

Alex nodded, trying not to cry. His shallow breath caught with the effort, and he groaned before he could stop it.

"Let's get the sedation started, Jeff."

"Not until Etan gets here," Alex said. "Please. I need to see him in case-"

"In case nothing." Sandy waved Jeff forward. "We're not putting you under yet. I'm not going to let you lie there in pain, either. This will let your muscles relax a little, that's all."

The nurse adjusted a tiny valve on a plastic tube running from a plastic bag filled with clear liquid into Alex's arm. He hadn't even noticed it. Another tube was attached to a different bag, the nearly black shade of the blood shocking in the harsh light.

Sandy focused on a silvery box on a small table near Alex's feet. Instead of a tube feeding into his bloodstream, the box trailed blue and green wires. They merged into a black cord that ended in a thick translucent patch the size of his palm. Full of tiny cables and colors, the patch lay flat against the opposite side of his ribs.

He had a vague, impossible-to-grasp memory of seeing the machine and the patch when their children were born.

"What is that?" he said, trying to look closer without hurting himself again. "Looks like some kind of circuitry."

"That's exactly what it is," Sandy said. "You'll know what it *does* in just a second."

She touched the box a few times, and Alex heard a soft click. The pain deep in his chest stopped in an instant. He let out what little breath he had in a humming sigh.

"Magic. What you have there is magic."

Sandy smiled and took Alex's hand.

"I can't disagree with you. That's got the pain blocked. When we're ready, I'll use a higher setting to put you under for surgery. Safer and easier than anesthesia, and the supply will never run out since you set us up with steady electricity. Smuggling this little beauty out of the hospital back in Chicago was a trick, but damn well worth it."

Alex nodded, closing his eyes.

"I'll say. Make sure I'm awake when Etan gets here."

Chapter 21

Etan drew back when he saw several people through the rows of floor to ceiling windows, waiting in the emergency lobby of the hospital. The gray and pale green space was normally empty, and usually closed unless there was an accident. Sandy usually worked out of a normal office on the other side of the three-story brick building for appointments.

The lights were on low, ticking and humming along with the generator. This one was set up in line with the massive water wheel in the Grasspe River a few blocks away. The generators that worked with the windmills up on Maple Ridge to supply the operating rooms were fueled by alcohol from the massive sugar beet crop they brought in every year.

All Alex's work, results of a months-long project helping Sandy get the hospital onto a sustainable footing.

Work that would hopefully help her save his life now.

"I'm so sorry, Etan."

"We'll do whatever we can."

"They said they may need more blood."

"Such a brave thing he did."

Etan nodded, unable to follow their words or do more than shake their hands as he walked through. His legs felt a hundred feet long, his feet wooden boxes he'd never seen before and couldn't understand.

Carmen, one of Sandy's nurses from Chicago, met him in the middle of the crowd. Her round, normally smiling face was tense and worried, her long wavy black hair caught back in a messy bun. She put an arm around Etan's waist.

"Thank you all," she said, raising her voice. "I'll be back with you for the next round in a few minutes. I've got to get Etan back. They're ready to start."

Etan let Carmen lead him through the double doors into a dim corridor.

"Is Alex still all right?" he said. His spinning brain shifted under him. "Why are you out here?"

"He's holding his own, but they need to get started. I'm handling the blood donations."

"Blood donations?"

"For Alex, honey," she said, opening another set of double doors with huge windows in them. "He's lost a lot already."

Before Etan could answer, he saw his husband on the surgical table. Everyone moving around him wore faded purple scrubs and hats, but Alex only had a white paper sheet pulled nearly up to his waist. The lights in here were steady and painfully bright. Carmen squeezed Etan's arm before she left.

Sandy spoke from beside him before Etan could get his mind or legs moving again.

"There you are. He's here, Alex." She took over for Carmen, taking his arm to lead Etan toward the table. "We're ready, great timing. Everything points toward his spleen, with luck not his lung. That's what I'm feeling in my gut, too."

"Carmen said they were giving blood for him," Etan said. "I want to donate."

"I'd be glad to let you," she said, "but in this one case you're not his type. He's O positive, you're A positive. We've got plenty on the way. You're going to need your strength. You can help next time."

"Etan," Alex whispered.

He was nearly as pale as the sheet, but vivid dark bruises stood out against the swollen skin of his abdomen. He lifted his fingers. Etan took his hand, forcing his eyes away from the cleaned wound, startled at how cold Alex's hand was.

"I'm here, sweetie. The kids are with Iris and Gena. Everything's going to be fine."

"Do they know? What's happening?"

"They know Doctor Sandy is taking great care of you. And they know you kept the monster from hurting Connor."

"Some savior, laying here flat on my back. Can you feel anything, E? Do you know if I'm going to make it?"

Etan bit the insides of his cheeks, hot, metallic blood flooding his mouth. Blood that couldn't help Alex.

If he'd seen the fucking Dream more clearly before it was too late, he wouldn't be standing here at all. His husband wouldn't be waiting for emergency surgery with people lined up in the lobby to try to help him through it.

"I don't see anything right now except our babies' hero." He kissed Alex's cool, bluish lips. "And mine. I'm waiting to see you back home in our bed."

"It's a date."

Sandy stood on Alex's other side, over the gash below his ribs. All the dark red hair was gone from that side, and she held a blue drape with a hole in the middle in her gloved hands. Etan forced himself to ignore the tubes and cables attached to Alex's body.

"We're ready," Sandy said. "We'll take good care of him, Etan. Hang in there. See you on the other side."

Chapter 22

Etan tried walking up and down the length of the pale blue tiled hall, but after Carmen took the fourth bag of blood into the operating room, he couldn't stand to know any more. He walked to the exit door and part of the way back, stopping before he could accidentally see where all that blood was going.

He wished for one of Alex's beloved watches, though he wasn't sure if keeping track of the time would make this better or worse. Even with a stopwatch or his long-dead smartphone, he had no idea how long a splenectomy was supposed to take. He hadn't thought to ask.

Squeaking shoes in the hallway got his attention, and he looked up before he could stop himself. Carmen was carrying two more bags of blood, her round face worried until she saw Etan. Her features shifted into a calm smile before she backed into the operating room.

Etan leaned against the white wall and sank to the floor.

He couldn't watch. He couldn't think. He couldn't do anything but wrap his arms around his knees and hide his face.

He fell into a half-Dream, not quite deep enough to shut out the cold hard tile under his backside or the wall against his spine.

Nowhere near deep enough to block out the twisting in his heart.

He saw himself and Alex, both of them barely Caela's age, holding hands and running through a rolling field of wheat. He felt the sun on his face, felt the grain tickling against his arms and legs. Etan felt Alex's hand, warm and firm in his own.

He saw them on an airplane, side by side peering out the tiny oval window, an adventure they'd only taken a few times before everything ended. A vast blue ocean stretched beneath them as far as he could see. Etan knew it was the Atlantic. That was a trip they'd talked and dreamed about, but never managed before it was too late.

He walked with his arm around Alex's waist, both of them with white hair and wrinkles on their faces. His husband's only held lines from smiling around his mouth and his gorgeous blue eyes. Their grown children, grandchildren, and great-grandchildren circled around them, laughing and playing.

"Please," he whispered. "Please give him back to me."

A hand on his shoulder jerked Etan back into hard reality.

Sandy stood beside him. She'd pulled off her gloves and her gown, but he saw spots of blood on the blue cloth booties covering her shoes. He stood as fast as he could to get away from it. Stiff muscles in his legs and back protested the sudden motion.

"Is it over?"

"He's hanging in there, Etan," she said, her voice weary. "Long road ahead, but we're past the crisis."

"Can I see him?"

"You can look in if you want, but he's still out. It takes a while to wake up after something like this."

"Do whatever you can to keep him from hurting," Etan said. "I can wait."

"It's not just that, hon. He had a rough time of it. So did we."

Etan's brow wrinkled and he rubbed the bridge of his nose. He wasn't sure he'd be able to hear the rest of what Sandy needed to tell him. And he knew Alex would never admit how badly he'd been hurt.

"Tell me."

Sandy leaned against the wall with a long sigh.

"The incision will be bigger than you expect. I couldn't have done this much smaller eleven years ago in a fully stocked hospital, not with how fast he was bleeding. But we had to take extra care in cleaning this wound out."

"He had one of the last tetanus shots," Etan said. "A couple of years ago."

"Right, that's a good thing. We have to watch for infections from how filthy the knife was, too. I repaired his diaphragm, but we had to take his entire spleen. He's going to have to watch for infections for the rest of his life, Etan."

"We still have some antibiotics, right?"

"We do, but what we have left won't last much longer. I'll give him a round for the next couple of weeks, and I'll give him the few immunizations we have left, too. What kind of patient will he be?"

Etan let out a laugh that sounded more like a groan.

"He's *terrible*," he said, leaning against the wall beside Sandy. "Worse than the kids. I've always been thankful he doesn't get sick much."

"Well, that may change. His immune system just took a big hit that takes a while to recover from. It would have been a lot more serious for Connor, but this is bad enough. We'll do everything we can to keep it to a minimum. The good news is he worked his ass off to give us a lot of other options when the drugs are gone, in the greenhouse and in the gardens. Will he eat garlic?"

"He hates it. All the rest of us love it."

"He's going to have to get over that," she said. She pulled out her usual small notebook that had to be one of the few left. "I'll make sure you get a supply of the larger bulbs, much milder flavor. We'll set some aside for you this autumn."

"I have to tell you he's going to hate *all* of this, Sandy. He didn't even want us to use fuel for the truck to bring him over here."

She scribbled a few lines, then stood upright and looked Etan in the eye.

"Again, he's going to have to get over it. He has to let us help him, and I'll need *you* to make sure that happens. If it weren't for the two of you, we wouldn't be standing here in a hospital room with lights and running water, worrying about which variety of garlic he'll choke down. Every last one of us would be dead or wishing we were. Alex has to let us take care of *him* for a change. Got it?"

"Got it. I can be more stubborn than Alex if it keeps him with us."

"Good." She wrote a few more lines before she closed the book. "With no infections or other problems, he's got at least a month, maybe closer to two before he starts to feel normal again. I'll get all of this written up and tell him myself so you won't be on your own. No picking up the kids or anything else, and they'll have to be careful of his incision."

"I'll definitely need help with that," Etan said. He saw Alex slinging Connor under his arm, lifting Meghan with no effort. The joy all of them took in the game and the affection. "None of them will be happy."

"I know, I've seen him with them. With any other kid, too. He'll have to let his body heal. *All* of you will need time to heal. We've got a few herbs that will help keep everyone calm, but it's going to take time and probably a lot of talking. Everyone will help if you'll let us. Understand?"

Etan looked down the hall toward the room where Alex waited, probably still too out of it to know what had happened. Getting himself and his husband through would pale beside trying to help their children believe their world was safe.

Especially since that was a lie Etan himself could never afford to believe again.

"I understand. We're going to have to take security more seriously once we deal with whoever that was."

"Mary's armed militia," Sandy said. She rubbed her upper arms. "I doubt anyone will argue now. I know I won't."

"How long do you think he'll sleep?" Etan said.

His heart had seized upon the next thing he had to do with the force of a Dream. He didn't want to give his reeling mind a chance to talk him out of it.

"Jeff is just about finished checking all his vitals, but with the e-sedation we can safely give you an hour before he's really aware. Whatever an hour means anymore. The rest will do him good if he's as bad as you say. He'll be staying here for at least a few days. Go out that back exit if you want privacy. I'll let everyone out front know Alex is okay."

"You'll get to see just what a rotten patient he is, then. Does someone have his things?"

"Yeah, they're in the OR," Sandy said. She touched his arm. "Do you want to go in? I can bring everything to you if you're not ready."

"I need to see him. At least for a second."

She linked her arm through his and they walked through the door together. Etan took a deep breath before he looked up.

A clean white sheet was pulled up to his husband's chin, thankfully covering his belly. His face was nearly as pale as the sheet, a horrible contrast to the red in his beard. Alex was still except for the slow rise and fall of his chest. Jeff looked up from the machine he was watching, nodding and smiling at Etan.

Sandy squeezed his arm for a second, then stepped away. Etan couldn't move. He wanted to get closer, to touch his lover's body, prove to himself that Alex was still alive. His own body wouldn't respond.

What if he passed along a head cold, some silly thing that would barely make him sneeze but proved fatal to Alex? How would he ever be sure enough that their kids' hands were clean enough to touch their father?

A simple sweet kiss could lead to an infection none of them would ever recover from.

He jumped when Sandy spoke.

"Here you go." She handed him one of the same fabric bags they used in the fields, this one made from threadbare blue jeans. "Everything's in there except his shirt. I can give it back if you want, or if Alex might."

"No, thank you for thinking of that," Etan said. "Hold on to it in case he wants it, but I don't."

He'd never get the spreading crimson stain on that faded blue t-shirt, Alex's fingers pressing into the bleeding gash in his side, out of his mind. He didn't ever want to see it again.

"I just need a couple of things."

Sandy watched him for a second, then took his arm again.

"He's good right now, Etan. Jeff and I will stay here until you get back, then we'll move him to a room. Go do what you need to."

Far from being reassured by Sandy's voice, Etan was chilled. Her eyes were worse, colder and harder than he'd ever seen them. He'd always thought her Dreams and visions focused on her patients, the general health of the community.

But right now he knew she saw exactly the same thing he did.

This was not a day for mercy or compassion.

Not anymore.

"I may need…" he said, hot sweat covering his body at the near confession of his plans. "In case someone's there."

Sandy crossed to the other side of the room and opened a wide metal drawer. He heard several taps against plastic. She returned and pressed an old brown prescription bottle and a shrink-wrapped syringe into his hand, angling her body so Jeff couldn't see.

"Crush these, then dissolve them in water. Ingestion or injection, there's no stopping it. And *no one* in this hospital would try."

He gazed into her blazing eyes, then nodded once. He dropped everything into his pocket.

Etan watched Alex long enough to see the steady rise and fall. He dug into the bag, leaving the dusty pants and shoes. He handed the rest back to Sandy.

He pulled off his wedding ring, then slipped it back on above Alex's larger version. He carefully lined up Anne's green stone set into each. Both of them together pinched his finger a little, but they wouldn't fall off. Etan fastened Alex's current black digital watch with a worn black leather band onto his wrist. It was loose, but not enough to fall off over his hand.

"An hour?"

"A bit longer if you need it. We'll tell him you're taking care of your children."

"I will be. Thank you, Sandy. For everything."

Chapter 23

Cool air against his face. A horrible taste in his mouth. And nothing hurt, not even a whisper.

Too vivid to be real, his sluggish mind whispered. Better enjoy it while it lasts.

Alex heard a soft click near his right ear, the same noise Sandy had somehow used to block his pain and send him into oblivion.

The sedation withdrew as quickly as it had come, the fog clearing in seconds. His senses shifted into clarity.

The hard table under his shoulders, the lingering sting of antiseptic in the room, all too mundane to be part of some kind of hallucination. Alex knew Sandy was worried about whatever she needed to do to him, but he couldn't remember why just yet.

Though he couldn't feel the painfully bright lights against his eyelids, Alex still squinted as he opened his eyes.

"Hey, Alex," a man said. Not Etan. "Don't worry, the lights are back to normal."

Alex blinked what felt like grit away, not much different than when he'd fallen asleep too hard after one of Etan's Dreams. Jeff sat beside him, still wearing the purple shirt, but without the hat or mask.

"How… how did it go?"

"Everything went fine," Jeff said, smiling. "You gave us a bit of a challenge, but we all feel good about it. Anything hurting?"

Alex closed his eyes for a second, trying to locate the various disconnected parts of his body. Back cool and stiff from the table. Head still a bit swimmy from Sandy's magic machine. Legs achy from being still so long. He frowned at the numbness, the lack of feeling from his armpits to below his waist.

"I still can't feel my chest. My stomach."

"But everything else is good?"

"Yeah, more or less."

"Well, that's by design," Jeff said. He held a straw to Alex's lips. The cold water was the best thing he'd ever tasted in his life. "We'll use the pain block until you're ready to go back home, maybe after that depending on how you're feeling."

"Are my lungs okay? Feels easier to breathe."

"That was a lucky break. The knife got your diaphragm, just like we thought. Didn't even scratch your lung, though. Getting your spleen out of the way made it a lot easier to repair the damage."

"There's the silver lining," Alex said. "Does Etan know?"

Jeff blinked and his lips compressed, so fast Alex wasn't sure he'd actually seen it.

Something didn't feel right. Not threatening, just strange.

"He does, Sandy talked to him. He had to go take care of your kids for a little while. He should be back any time now."

"Any chance you'll tell me what Etan's really up to?"

Jeff grinned, shaking his head.

"Yeah, you're pretty damn awake. Not a chance that I will. Mainly because I don't know. You'll need to ask him yourself."

Chapter 24

Etan kept to the alley behind the cinderblock hospital, walking between it and a bunch of red and brown brick buildings. Sandy's advice was accurate and welcome. The late afternoon was usually a fairly busy time. Today no one was out, at least not that he could see.

The town jail had seen surprisingly little use since the end of the old world. The brick building Etan remembered from his childhood had been replaced with a modern blue vinyl-sided version years before, jarring against the rest of the original structures on the edge of town.

Etan had only been inside the new building a couple of times, back at the beginning of the end. Random drunken brawls as news filtered in of how bad things were going to get died down within a few months.

After the raiders from Maple Ridge, everyone understood there were too few people left to spend all that time and energy trying to destroy each other.

Etan had tried to convince everyone, including Alex, that ending a human life when almost all of them were gone was the closest thing they had to a sin. Up until that morning, he'd still felt that way.

He hoped he'd recover that belief in everything they were struggling for.

Maybe around the time the scars on his husband's belly faded.

The glass front door of the jail was unlocked, and Etan saw a faint yellow light inside. He hadn't even thought to ask where they'd brought the monster that attacked Connor and then Alex. Nowhere else made sense.

Harry Mullins stood up from behind a cluttered wooden desk.

"Etan. How's Alex? Come through the surgery okay?"

"He's hanging in there, Harry. He's going to have a long recovery, but that may be harder on the rest of us than on him."

"Glad to hear it. Listen, I'm real sorry about what happened today. Guess all of us need to take Mary's crazy militia idea a little more seriously."

Etan leaned against the chest-high counter opposite the desk, hoping the pills didn't rattle in his pocket.

"I'm not even sure she ever Dreamed that, you know?" he said. "She wasn't exactly thrilled with the little bit we did talk about it. But we'll have to talk about it now. At least when we have people out in the fields."

"I know a woman who'd be perfect to take charge of all that." Harry rubbed his chin. "Got a good feeling about how she'd work out. Don't mean to be rude, but what the hell you doing down here?"

"I need to see whoever did this, Harry. I need to know why."

"Whoever that used to be can't tell you much, son. She's skin and bones, half wild and more than half starved to death."

"She, huh?" Etan said. That made no difference to him at all, not after what she'd tried to do to Connor and Alex. But he knew it made a lot of difference to some people. "She tried to take our son, and she nearly killed Alex. All I'm asking for is to see her."

Harry took a deep breath, tilting his head as he studied Etan.

"You know there may be a lot more of them out there," he said slowly. "This one may be the key to learning more about that."

"I don't doubt there are more out there. This one doesn't know enough about them to help us. She's by herself. No one to report back to."

"Dreamed about it, did you? I'm real sorry to sound so harsh, but when was that?"

Etan forced his mind to be still, to not turn and bite and claw itself with guilt. That wouldn't make all of this go away, no matter how badly he tore himself up.

"I didn't see it until this morning. I wish to hell it had been sooner, but I saw it just a few minutes before it happened."

"I thought so," Harry said. He walked out from behind the desk and stood beside Etan. "That's what bothers me most. We got a town full of goddamn fortune tellers, and not a one of us saw this thing coming. We can't let that happen again."

"You're right. We can't. *I* can't."

Harry put one arm around Etan.

"You sure about this?"

"I'm sure as I can be after the worst day of my life."

"Well, all I'll say is make sure you're not about to make it worse, Etan. Make *real* sure of that."

Harry left a key ring and a small black handgun on the high counter before he went out the door.

Another piece of Etan's vision slipped into place.

Harry didn't look back when Etan turned the deadbolt.

None of these buildings on the edge of town had running water. Pretty much only the hospital, the greenhouse and cannery, and the Council apartments did. Alex and a few others hoped to get that expanded, but who knew how long that would take now?

Almost every building had a few containers of water inside, though, filtered from rain or the river and stored away. Behind the high counter, Etan found a broad, white ceramic jar that must have been the base for a water bottle when such things were still delivered. Luxury none of them had known to think twice about.

He pulled the lid off and picked up two of the navy blue coffee mugs still lined up around the cooler. He filled one for himself, drained it, then filled and drained it again. He hadn't realized until that moment that he'd never gotten anything to eat or drink since the nightmare drove him out into the morning hours ago.

Etan poured all seven of the pills into the other mug, using a spoon out of the sugar container to crush them. A crust of sparking white lined the jar, so he scraped all of it out and dumped it in before he poured water in and stirred.

Shame to waste any kind of sweetness here, but he'd take any shortcut he could get.

After one more long drink of the cool water, almost the last in the jar, he replaced the lid and picked up Harry's lantern.

The syringe was still in his pocket, but he hoped he wouldn't need it.

Etan stared at the handgun, trying to remember the last time he'd held one. Probably when he and his father took Alex target shooting when they first moved back. Again, the luxury of using up bullets for fun was hard to imagine.

He popped the magazine into his hand, made sure it was loaded, and clicked it back into place. Etan flipped the safety off, then back on before he slipped it into his back pocket.

Badly as he needed to go through with this, he had no intention of risking his own life on the day they'd almost lost Alex.

The cell row was just inside a thick wooden door. Six bleak concrete rooms with doors made of metal bars on the front, and only the first one locked closed. Etan stood for a long time watching the woman inside lying on the bed. He wouldn't have been able to tell by looking that she was female.

He could hardly tell she was human.

Her hair was long and matted, her clothes barely qualified as rags. Her hands, face, and feet were so filthy she seemed to have shoes, gloves, and a mask on.

When Etan unlocked the cell, she sat straight up, staring at him.

"Relax," he said, leaving the lantern on the floor outside the cell. "I just want to talk to you."

She drew her feet up onto the bed, but she never took her eyes off Etan. He didn't know if Harry and the others had pushed her hair back or if he'd been too upset to notice, but up close her features were obviously feminine. Small jaw and nose, high cheekbones. The snarling rage he'd seen directed at Connor and Alex overrode everything else.

He stepped inside the shadowy cell.

"Are you thirsty?"

Her eyes darted to the mug he carried, then back to his face.

"Just tell me why you were there today. I need to know what happened."

She only watched him.

"Are there others like you? Out in the woods? Someone you're trying to take care of?"

Her eyes narrowed, but she was silent.

"Here, just drink the water. Maybe you'll feel more like talking."

She looked down at his hands again, and he wondered if she noticed the rings he wore, the facets of white gold flickering in the lantern light.

He wondered if she understood why he was wearing two of them.

Etan's voice dropped to a menacing whisper.

"What were you going to do with the little boy?"

She drew back, blinking. Etan stepped closer, keeping his body between her and the door.

"If you can still talk, you'll be a lot better off answering my questions. See, I'm all for keeping things as civil as we possibly can. That's what I've spent the last eleven years of my life trying to do."

He leaned forward and put the mug on a steel table built into the cinderblock wall. Her eyes followed his hand.

"What you did today is exactly what I'm trying to keep from happening. I need to understand how we can do that."

She looked back at Etan, but she leaned forward slowly, reaching for the water.

"What's your name?"

She scowled as she picked up the mug, sniffing at the water. Etan held his breath.

He hadn't noticed a smell from the pills, but he hadn't been looking for one.

She settled back onto the bed, holding the mug in both hands.

"My name is Etan Griffith."

The woman sipped the water. She jerked her head back and glared at Etan.

"It's sugar. Probably the last refined sugar in this part of the world."

She drank slowly, then more deeply.

"My husband's name is Alex Collins," he said, his heart beating faster with every movement of her throat. "Our son's name is Connor. He was named after my father, who never got to meet him. Thieves killed my father. Strangers who wanted to steal from us and hurt us instead of working with us, letting us help them."

She held the empty mug in both hands, watching him.

"I wish you *would* talk, to tell you the truth. I think you understand me though, so that will have to do."

Etan squatted, noticing the woman moved more slowly when she drew back. If she'd taken Sandy's pills on a long-empty stomach, this whole thing could be over in minutes.

"I truly am sorry you're in such a state. I wish you'd come to us a long time ago, or gone to someone else. We took in as many people as we could, even from Maple Ridge, and we still help everyone we can."

He shifted and drew the gun behind his back, flipping the safety off. Her eyes tracked his movements a split-second behind.

"There's no way I can help you now, though. I don't know what you were trying to do with Connor, and I don't care. We should put you on trial and try to figure that out. But we're not going to."

The woman blinked several times, then looked down at the mug she still held.

"You gave up your chance for help when you tried to take my son. And you earned this when you almost killed my husband."

Etan brought the gun around, holding it pointed at the floor. The woman blinked again, looking from the gun back into his eyes.

"I want to shoot you through the heart and be finished with it. But that's not what I saw. I saw myself giving you the choice between the gun and just lying down and going to sleep. I couldn't see past that. You're not going to see another day, but I won't dishonor my own vision no matter how much I want to. The choice is yours."

Chapter 25

The lights were still on in the emergency lobby of the hospital when Etan returned, but no one was inside.

Except one man, once again sitting behind a desk.

"Harry."

"Etan. Everything's fine here."

"Everything's fine with me, then."

Harry stood, his broad shoulders more stooped than Etan remembered from less than an hour ago. Forty-two minutes according to Alex's watch.

"Anything I need to know before I head back?"

"Starvation is a terrible thing. So is dying alone."

Etan dropped the keys into Harry's hand as the older man walked past.

"Let me know if I can do anything to help with Alex or the kids," Harry said as he stepped outside. "Or you."

"Thank you. I will."

Harry never asked about the gun in Etan's pocket, still fully loaded.

Sandy and Jeff sat on a gurney close by the operating table. Alex was still far too pale, but he looked up as soon as Etan walked in.

His smile was all the absolution Etan needed.

Chapter 26

ALEX COULDN'T REMEMBER BEING MORE grateful for a soft bed in his entire life. Softer than the operating table, at least, and that was more than enough.

The lights in the room weren't nearly as blinding, either. They were dim enough that he wasn't quite sure if the walls were the same soothing blue as the rest of the hospital.

Another bed sat on the other side of the room. Etan slumped in the middle of it, face nearly as pale as the walls but definitely not soothing.

"Etan, you're about to fall over," Alex said. "Just lie down and close your eyes."

"I'm fine," Etan said, shaking his head. "I'll rest when I know you're settled for the night. Do you need anything?"

"Besides not worrying about you? I'm freezing."

"That's the hangover from the full block," Sandy said from the doorway. She opened a closet by the window. "Pretty much the only side effect. Unfortunately the pain block we're still using can make that worse."

She covered the thin white sheet pulled up to his chin with a thick brown blanket, then glanced at the silvery box hanging on the wall above the bed.

The magic box.

"We can start reducing the block over the next day or so, but I'd rather have you a bit chilly than in pain. Need me to turn the mattress heat on?"

Alex frowned, once again checking past the odd numb sensation of his chest. His legs ached terribly, and he felt like he should be shivering. The sensation of an involuntary movement that couldn't happen was strangely disorienting.

"Yeah, crank it up." He caught Etan's head drooping out of the corner of his eye. "Sleepyhead over there is the one who likes to be cold."

"You got it." She touched the screen over Alex's head, just out of his sight. "Etan, you're asleep sitting up."

"So Alex tells me," he said with a half smile. "I can sleep here if that's okay."

"That's not my call," Sandy said, her own smile was mischievous. "Someone else has strong opinions on the subject, and I'm not about to cross her."

She stepped out into the hall for a few seconds. Laura Griffith peeked around the doorway.

"Mind if I come in?"

"Of course not," Etan said. He stood and caught his mother in a hug. "I'm so glad you're here."

She turned to Alex, her eyes bright and sad. Laura looked ready for bed, long silver and blonde hair pulled into a braid, wearing the same soft pajamas covered with songbirds that she wore for frequent sleepovers with her grandchildren.

"Does anything hurt, hon?" she said, kissing Alex on the forehead.

Tears made Alex's eyes ache nearly as much as his legs. His own mother had rarely shown so much affection, not even when he was Caela's age.

"Not with Sandy's magic box," he said. "She's even got my ass warming up so I'll stop complaining."

"Good. You just tell me if anything bothers you at all. Etan, go home."

Etan snorted and shook his head. He winked at Alex. Alex found the tiniest of lighthearted gestures from his husband helped more than all the pain medication in the world.

"You wouldn't think I was thirty-three years old with kids of my own, would you?" Etan said. "I'd swear my mother just told me to go home."

"That's *exactly* what I just told you." Laura sat beside Etan. "Alex is in the best place he could possibly be, and you're about done in. You look the same as when you played out in the snow too long as little boy. I'll watch over him, sweetheart. You go home to my grandbabies."

Alex watched the two of them, wondering how Etan could believe it was worth arguing with his mother with that tone in her voice.

"Maybe you could stay with them, Mom," Etan said. His own soft voice made it clear he knew it was no use. "They're always happy to see you."

"I *did* just see them, son. They're fine, but they're scared to death. They need Daddy E while they're so worried about Daddy A."

"That does make sense," Alex said. He noticed Sandy in the doorway this time. "Sandy said I'm going to be asleep soon anyway. I'll be home getting on your nerves soon enough."

"That you will," she said. "I'll be right next door. I pretty much have an apartment set up, almost as comfortable as my house."

Etan groaned, but he let Laura pull him to his feet. He brushed Alex's hair back. Alex caught his hand and kissed it.

"What do you want me to do, sweetie?" Etan said.

"I must still be knocked out," Alex said, grinning at his mother-in-law. "I'd swear Etan just asked me what I want him to do. First time in fourteen years."

"Jackass," Etan said under his breath. "How's he doing, Sandy? Physically, I mean."

"Everything looks good. He needs rest more than anything else right now. Laura's right. You're run ragged. Seeing your kids will do you and them a world of good. We'll both be right here with Alex."

Etan crossed his arms, drumming his fingers against his biceps. He looked at each of them in turn, then last at Alex.

"It's fine, E," Alex said. "I'll be sound asleep in a minute anyway. You'll *all* feel better at home, and I will too knowing you're with our kids."

Chapter 27

Etan knocked on the door to Iris and Gena's apartment barely ten minutes later, hoping all their children were asleep. He was too early for their normal bedtime, but this had not been a normal day. Gena opened the door a crack, her blonde hair and one eye barely visible past the chain Etan had never seen her use.

His heart ached at such an antiquated notion, as if locked doors would keep the monsters away ever again.

"Etan, hon, come on in. Laura just left, she said Alex came through the surgery."

She pushed the door closed, then opened it wide. He had time to relax into her hug, her warmth, for a few seconds before he took in the room behind her.

Iris sat on the floor, surrounded by nine children. All of them awake. All of them staring at him with their eyes wide and afraid. Caela jumped to her feet and ran over to him.

"Where's Daddy Alex?"

Before Etan could answer, all of their children thundered toward him. Iris picked Eddie up when the youngest of them started crying as his brothers and sisters left him behind. Etan knelt, holding his arms out to gather all of them as close as he could.

"Daddy Alex is staying at Dr. Sandy's for a little while," he said.

"She's going to help him get all better. He misses you, and he asked me to tell every one of you how much he loves you."

All of them started talking at once, and Iris and Gena tried their best to keep everyone calm. Their children who lived down here with their mothers adored Alex just as much as the five he and Etan were raising.

Caela stood beside Etan, her hand on his shoulder as the younger ones clamored for his attention. He turned to her.

"How long does he have to stay there?" she said, her tiny brow wrinkled.

"We're not sure, baby. For a few days at least."

"Will someone watch out for him and make sure he's safe?"

"Dr. Sandy will be right there," Etan said. "She's taking really good care of him. Your Gramma is with him, too."

"Do Dr. Sandy and Gramma know to watch out for the bad thing so it won't hurt Daddy Alex again?"

Etan knew, in the clearest flash of intuition he or any of the other Dreamers would have for months, that Caela would need to know the truth about what he'd done someday. He'd have to tell Alex as well, and a hell of a lot sooner.

He couldn't see why, but he knew their daughter would need that knowledge for a deeper reason than satisfying her curiosity. And he knew that day was safely distant, years in the future.

"The bad thing is gone," he said. The distressed voices of their children fell silent at his words. "The bad thing is gone, and it can't ever hurt anyone again."

"Go see Daddy A?" Connor said. He was leaning on Etan's thighs and against his chest, his fine brown hair sweet from a recent bath.

"Not yet," Gena said. She knelt beside Etan, her hand on his other shoulder. "Maybe in a few days."

"Dr. Sandy will tell us when we can go see him," Iris said. She swayed back and forth with Eddie droopy-eyed in her arms. Etan wished he could join their son in that safe embrace.

"We'll all have to be extra careful when we do," he said, looking at each of them in turn. "He's getting better, but we don't want to hurt him or make him sick. We'll talk more about that when it's time."

"Are you hungry, Etan?" Gena said. "We have plenty here. People have been bringing food all day."

"I'm starving, but I'm about to fall asleep on my feet. I'll get our bunch rounded up and head upstairs."

Iris kissed Eddie's head and smiled.

"Don't be ridiculous, Daddy E. You'll eat while we get the kids settled in together. Then you'll stay here with us for as long as you need to. No arguments. You know it's the only thing that makes sense."

Etan's breath caught, and he hid his face against Connor's soft hair. It hadn't occurred to him yet how awful it was going to be, sleeping in their bed without Alex. Trying to pretend everything was all right for their children's sake while trying to keep his mind from flaying his heart to bits.

"I'd love that," he said, looking up. "We all would."

The younger kids followed their mothers without too much complaining, but Caela hung back. Etan nodded at Iris, then held out his arms to their oldest, catching her in a strong hug.

"Want to stay in here with me while I eat?" he said. "Are you hungry?"

"I'm not hungry, Daddy E. We ate a whole bunch. Can I ask you something?"

Etan stood with her, surprised at how heavy she was when he was so weary. That was something else that had never occurred to him. In a few short years, he wouldn't be able to pick Caela up anymore.

He hoped Alex would be able to lift her again before she got too big.

"You can ask me anything, baby."

She sat at the long wood plank table where they often shared meals while he roamed around the kitchen, piling two plates with enough food to make up for his three missed meals and a little bit more.

Caela held her chin in her hands and stared at him when he sat beside her.

"What did Dr. Sandy do? About the cut in Daddy A's belly?"

"She fixed it up," Etan said, glad he hadn't started eating yet. "It will take a little while, but he's going to be fine."

"Did she sew it? Like our clothes?"

Etan nodded, smiling at her quickness even as his empty stomach protested.

"She did. Pretty cool, huh?"

"I guess. Is that why we have to be so careful?"

"That's why. We don't want to hurt his belly. We'll have to wash our hands even more than usual, too, so we don't make him sick."

Caela watched him eat, her mouth pursed and her fingers drumming on the table. Etan wondered how often Alex's parents sat with their nearly identical little boy doing exactly the same thing.

"If he gets sick, he'll have to stay at Dr. Sandy's longer, won't he?" she finally said.

"You're right. We want him home as soon as possible, so we'll have to do everything we can to help him get better."

"Even if that means no playtime."

"For a while, yeah, sweetheart. No playtime with Daddy A. You can have playtime with me, though. I know I'm not as much fun, but I'll do my best."

Caela stared at him, her pale eyebrows raised. Etan had never felt so thoroughly examined and evaluated.

"Okay. I'll teach you. Night, Daddy E. Love you."

She kissed his cheek and walked away.

"Night, Caela. Love you," he said, then continued under his breath. "Alex loves you, too."

Iris and Gena came in just as he finished the absurd amount of food. Etan didn't feel overly full, but the gnawing in his belly was gone for the first time all day.

"Come on, Etan," Gena said, holding out her hand. Etan stood and held on tight. "We'll get this tomorrow. Time to go to bed."

"Anything change with Alex while you were there?" Iris said.

"He's stable right now. Mom's staying in the room with him,

Sandy next door. The next couple of weeks will be the hardest. If he…" Etan stumbled – the words and the reality of how much ground his husband still had to cover robbing the tiny bit of strength he had left. "Once he gets through that, things will be easier."

Etan didn't protest when Iris and Gena pulled off his shoes and clothes. His breath hitched in his throat twice before they finished. When they settled in on either side of him, each with an arm across his chest, he gave in to the tears he'd been fighting since the Dream ripped through his mind.

He'd never slept with Iris and Gena without Alex, the four of them spent and satisfied, hoping another life would join their family. Another chance at eternity, at a future for humanity.

Their warmth and comfort that night kept him from flying apart, helped him sleep when he thought he'd never be able to again.

Chapter 28

ALEX HELD Etan's hand tight as they walked toward the storage shed at the edge of the old football field. Months of rain and weather, harvest and replanting had long since washed away the footprints, and the blood. All of the plants out there had young, early summer vigor rather than the near slumber of October.

Yet he knew he'd always be able to spot exactly where he'd nearly lost his life.

Two of the red hound dogs ranged ahead of them, noses to the ground, but without the urgency they'd shown that terrible day. Their warning may have led Alex to that encounter with a knife in his belly, but they'd prevented what could only have been far worse if one of the students walked in there instead.

Or one of their children.

He couldn't see Dana Chen, their new head of security, or any of her armed guards. Alex knew they were there, especially with him wandering around out here at dusk. He was already growing weary of so much attention coming his way.

He couldn't sigh or twitch or cough without someone asking if he was okay.

And still, the shadows deepening in the woods beyond the field seemed to crawl up his legs, making his balls draw up tight and try to disappear. Alex was as uneasy as he'd been the first few weeks after they'd moved from Chicago to Virginia. He couldn't see anything specific, but everything that creaked or groaned or shifted felt like a threat to him.

The structures and paths and patterns Alex had depended on for most of his life had deserted him, with the students and his children as Witnesses.

His sense of the shape and boundaries of his life had shattered, leaving him more vulnerable and afraid than he'd ever been.

As he so often did, Etan voiced his thoughts before Alex could find the words.

"Maybe we shouldn't be out here yet, sweetie."

Alex looked around one more time, turning in a slow circle. He wished for the coarse comfort of his gun on his hip, though it would have dragged too much on his weak muscles. He glanced down yet again to make sure Etan carried his.

"Probably not, but I'm sick of being scared. I need to see it."

He was grateful when Etan put his arms around him, carefully, so carefully. Alex's face twisted when he realized Etan was turning them, angling their bodies so *he* could still see out into the woods with the shed at his back. Neither of them had been so fearful and timid less than a year ago. He was afraid neither of them would ever recover.

"What did you see, Etan? Not in your Dream. I mean what did you see here? I know you've told me more than once, but I need to hear you where I can see it all for myself."

He felt Etan's chest rise and fall slowly. He leaned back and touched Alex's cheek with his fingertips. Checking for fever, of course. A stubborn infection in Alex's wound had led to more surgeries, then a dreadful struggle with pneumonia that knocked his recovery back even more. He understood how it all made Etan's overly protective impulse worse, but the effect was no less frustrating.

Alex worried that Etan would never stop, and that both of them would only grow more resentful with the constant attention over time.

Partly because he was so deeply afraid himself.

"Let me get a lantern, then sit down with me," Etan said. "I'll tell you what I remember as many times as you need me to."

Alex watched Etan unlock the heavy padlock on the door, unable to breathe until he stepped back outside with a lantern from their stores, then re-locked the door. He didn't want to ask and confirm it, but he was certain Etan wanted to make sure the shed was empty more than he wanted the light.

Alex would have done the same, and he probably always would.

His knees were weak enough between fear and the walk out here that he sat on the low porch rather than argue about it. The dogs settled down on the ground at their feet with exaggerated sighs.

Etan took Alex's hand in both of his. "Honestly, the line between the Dream and what I really saw has only gotten more blurry. I woke up with the whole thing screaming through my mind, took the kids to Iris and Gena, and ran. I guess it was all memory until I made it over the hill back there by the cannery."

Both of them looked at a rustle off to their right. The dogs didn't move. A yellow light that had to be another lantern grew brighter around the contour of the hill, but Alex's flesh crawled until he recognized the woman carrying it.

Dana, personally overseeing his security after all. She raised a hand and kept walking.

"I saw you going toward it right before it fell and you grabbed Connor," Etan said, then he shook his head. "*She*, not *it*. I couldn't tell that day, not then. I saw Connor get away. And I saw her stab you."

Alex's stomach twisted and heaved. He squeezed his eyes closed, desperate to keep his dinner where it belonged. Throwing up would be pure agony. And yet another sign of his weakness.

"All of you saw her stab me," he said, his jaw tight. "Our *children* saw that. Caela still wakes up screaming and I can't even pick her up to make it stop."

"Yes they did, sweetie. They saw you doing everything you could to keep Connor safe. They see you back home with us now, getting stronger every single day. Caela's nightmares are getting better over time, just like we thought they would."

The forest was nearly black now, and the early summer noises were louder. Alex remembered feeling this way thirteen years ago looking out at the trees and brush around their house in the middle of the woods. Nothing was ever so unknown, so mysterious and dark, in the suburbs of his Wisconsin childhood or in Chicago where he'd met Etan.

He'd known then as clearly as he knew now that humans were at the mercy of whatever moved in that darkness. Even more so now, as the defenses of bright lights, terrifying noise, and machines to chew through the wilderness fell away from the earth.

They once again huddled around campfires and inside their shelters, hoping the wild things weren't bold enough to break through that fragile circle of safety.

Alex had always hated lies, but he hated the unknown even more.

"What happened after that?" he said. "After the surgery? I know you went to the jail, Etan."

"That doesn't matter," Etan said. He shifted away long enough to light the lantern, then put his arm around Alex's shoulders. "She's gone. She'll never hurt you or our family again."

"It *does* matter, how can you say that? All of us are having nightmares. I don't know when you or I or our children will ever feel safe again. She's still hurting us, right this second."

"Let's go back home," Etan said. Alex heard the strain in his husband's voice, felt it in the tighter muscles in his arm. "Maybe we can talk more somewhere else."

"No, Etan, no! Tell me now. She'll keep slicing both of us up as long as we let her. Every time I imagine it for myself the cut gets deeper."

Alex pressed his fingers into the flesh under his ribs, trying to ease the pain. Shouting when his diaphragm was barely knitted back together and his lungs were still weak from pneumonia wasn't the smartest thing he'd ever done, not even compared to walking into this goddamn shed that morning.

But just like the stubborn infection he'd struggled so hard to fight through, the poison had to get out somehow.

Etan watched him, his face tight and worried.

"I did what I had to do to keep walking around when I didn't know if you ever would again. That's all."

"Then tell me what happened, E. No one else will. I think I deserve to know. At least tell me if another bunch of them is going to come out of those woods after her. Don't make me check over my shoulder for the rest of my life."

"She's dead, Alex. Probably starvation. I didn't see any others in my Dream that showed up too fucking late. She was alone. Dana's patrols will take care of any others out there."

"We don't know that. No one else had a Dream in time, either." Alex ran his hand along Etan's thigh, his old distraction trick that he knew wouldn't work at the moment. He did it for his own comfort rather than his husband's arousal. "I need to know. I'm not used to having nightmares. I don't know how you stand it almost every night. If I know what happened to her, they might stop."

"Mine never have. No one's Dreaming at all anymore, not the Dreams we need. Maybe we will again now that you're getting better. I can stand my nightmares because you're beside me every night."

Etan closed his eyes for several seconds. "I'm afraid of what you'll think of me."

"Then *listen* to me," Alex said. "The only thing I have any right to say is thank you if you were involved. I would have taken care of the problem if I'd been able to get up off that hospital bed. You know that. And you know I'll just keep asking until you get sick of hearing it."

"Okay, Alex. Okay. I did go back and talk to her, yes. And she did pass away while I was there."

"Natural causes, right?" Alex said, his eyes following another one of those patrol lanterns, the person carrying it hidden in the darkness. "Please don't lie to me."

The silence dragged out long enough that Alex thought he'd have to truly start begging. He didn't want to try to sleep again, to go willingly into the horror movies playing over and over in his mind until he dragged himself back to consciousness.

Not without knowing the truth.

Etan shifted until he sat cross-legged facing Alex. He moved the lantern between them, and Alex turned so he could watch his husband's face.

Whatever horrors waited for them beyond this faint circle of light would have to find satisfaction elsewhere.

"Right after Sandy came out and told me you made it through the surgery, I had a vision. I saw myself standing over the creature that attacked you, holding a gun in one hand and poison in the other. I knew I was meant to give her a choice. She could take the poison or I could shoot her."

"What did you do?" Alex whispered.

"I didn't quite give her that much of a choice." Etan's attempt to smile hurt Alex's heart. "I gave her poison, then told her I'd shoot her or she could lie down and go to sleep. I don't know if she decided, or if the poison kicked in. She was starved enough that it could have been that fast. Either way, I stood there until I knew she was dead. I'm not proud, but I was satisfied when she drew her last breath. Then I got back to you as fast as I could."

Etan stared into Alex's eyes, not flinching or drawing away. He was simply waiting.

"I wish you hadn't gone through that," Alex said. He didn't bother trying to hide his tears. "I never wanted you or our children to go through anything like that. *I'm* supposed to be the one keeping the monsters away."

Etan smiled. Not much, but it was real.

"Why's that, Alex? Because you're older, or more of a butch man than me, or some other such bullshit?"

"No, not even a little bit. Because you're the better of us. No one in this whole town would be here if it weren't for you. You've shown us the way more times than any of us can count."

"You know I still can't remember the Dreams, right? And no one puts these things together better than you do. Without that record-keeping and making connections and paying attention, all the

Dreams in the world wouldn't matter. Without you, I would have been too lonely, or too crazy, to have the damn Dreams a long time ago."

Alex didn't have the heart, or the energy, to argue. He *had* felt protective of Etan since the night they'd met, and that would never change. Not even when his own body was still too weak to even pick up their children.

He'd never wanted Etan to do something so hard, so cruel. An act that would change his gentle nature.

Etan reached up and touched Alex's cheek, but the caress was different now. Not only for comfort or reassurance, not anymore. The balance between them - gentle and strong, protective and perceptive - was altered forever. Alex didn't yet know what that shift would mean for them or the shape of their lives.

He took his own comfort in seeing that pattern again, sensing connection and motion all around them, for the first time since he'd last been in this field. The clouds of fireflies in the trees and on the ground aligned with the billions of stars above them, so many more than they'd imagined less than twenty years ago.

All of them turned and sang together with the rhythm of Alex's heart.

"Thank you for telling me, E," he said, leaning forward for a kiss. Much to his surprise, the catch under his ribs was a bit lighter. So was his heart. "And thank you for what you did. I know that wasn't easy. I probably wouldn't have been so kind."

Chapter 29

THE APARTMENT WAS QUIET, their bedroom dark, with all the children and probably everyone else in the building asleep. Alex held Etan's head, trying to keep him from drawing away. They'd never gone as long as a couple of weeks without making love before the attack.

Healing belly and weak muscles or not, he was climbing the walls with wanting his husband.

And with needing to feel normal again.

"Are you sure?" Etan whispered, his breathing as fast as Alex's.

"I'm sure. Sandy's sure. Nothing hurts anymore, E. I want you. It's been way too damn long."

Etan ran his fingers down Alex's chest, across the ticklish hair and over to the still-growing stubble on the other side. His light touch along the thick scars felt hot, like the nerves hadn't quite healed yet. The muscles hadn't yet either, still aching deep inside when he moved a certain way or coughed too hard.

Alex was determined to keep that much to himself.

"I don't want to hurt you," Etan said, pressing his hand flat over the scars. "We almost lost you."

Alex forced himself to breathe slowly, deliberately. It was one thing to be frustrated and moving into angry at how gingerly everyone was treating him, as if he were made of glass. Another thing entirely, and far worse, to let his own upset push away the person he needed most.

"No one knows that better than I do," he said, covering Etan's hand with his own. "I can't imagine anything worse than leaving our babies while they still need me so much, leaving you alone. Unless it's having all of you act like I'm not alive, not me, when I *am*."

He moved Etan's hand higher, over his pounding heart.

"I'm right here, Etan. I feel like a ghost everyone's afraid to touch or look at. Even our kids are afraid to hug me. I barely feel like I exist anymore. I need to feel like myself, not some pathetic invalid. I need you to *touch* me, and not like you're nursing me back to health."

Alex pulled Etan's head down and whispered, his lips against his ear.

"Touch me the way you used to. The way I used to touch you. Take me. Take every part of me. Like you're starving to death for me. Like your life depends on it."

"It does," Etan said. He groaned when Alex moved his hand from his heart to his straining cock. Alex nearly came with the heat and pressure of his lover's fingers after too much time. "I *am* starving to death for you."

"Then prove it. Make me feel it. You're not going to hurt me. Not unless you stop."

Etan kissed him again, softly at first, then hard enough to bruise Alex's lips. Alex didn't dare draw away, and he didn't want to. He squeezed Etan's body against his own, the aching heat in his chest only driving him on.

Etan wasn't the only one who needed to get over being afraid of infection, of scars. Of tearing open wounds no one could see anymore, and those no one could ever see.

Alex was choking to death, not on healing flesh but a half-lived life, too careful and rigid and cool.

Using his body the way it was meant to be used, even if that catch in his ribs lingered longer because of it, was the only way either of them could get close to normal life again.

Etan took both of them a long way toward normal that night.

Chapter 30

ALEX CHARGED up the concrete steps to their apartment, not fast enough to be called running. Not just yet. He'd started this little game with himself a few weeks after he and Etan had visited the fields where he'd been attacked, every time he managed to get to the ground floor unattended. Determined to rebuild his strength on his own terms.

He hadn't even pretended to argue about needing the old hand-crank elevator at first. His family would have had to move down to the first floor otherwise, especially once the pneumonia set in. Alex had despaired for a long time of even having the energy to turn the damn crank, much less climb the stairs under his own steam.

The first several attempts had him running out of breath at a slow walk, stopping several times on the way up, grasping his loose jeans to keep them on his hips. After weeks of having to slow down after one flight, then two, he was finally making it to the fourth floor without breathing too heavily. And his clothes weren't two sizes too big anymore.

His triumph was no less sweet for being private. Neither Etan nor Sandy would have approved. That alone, taking charge of his own body, did as much good for Alex's attitude as for his legs and heart.

The return of Etan's Dreams after nearly a year gave Alex even more reason for his solitary exercise. Gena's suggested weekly meetings among the Witnesses three years ago, right after Connor was born, helped Alex keep a hold on his sanity. Back then, comparing their journals let them see similarities developing, or other Dreamers sharing one of Etan's Dreams months later.

The strict rule preventing any of the Dreamers from attending, or reading each other's journals, assured them all that the Dreams were pure.

During the long time of no one Dreaming, they'd focused on standardizing their records, making sure they'd be useful for years into the future. When their children, grandchildren, and hopefully more might need to study their first tentative steps and stumbles.

Those long months of feeling blind tested more than Alex's patience, certainly. But he was equally certain he was the only one who felt he'd somehow caused the temporary blindness. And so his relief – as not only the Dreams themselves but all of Wolf Branch's *faith* in those Dreams recovered – buoyed Alex like floating in warm water.

He walked slowly down the hall toward their apartment, breathing deeply to hide any signs of his exertion. He hadn't even broken a sweat this time. His smile when he opened the door was genuine, as much for his own accomplishment as for the news he was excited to share.

"Daddy A," Gwen cried, jumping up from what looked like a terribly serious game of marbles. "Caela lost another tooth!"

Alex knelt, groaning at the deep stretch in his long thigh muscles, as everyone but their oldest daughter ran to greet him.

"Did she?" Alex said from the middle of the scrum. "We'll have to borrow money from the tooth fairy at this rate."

He saw Caela roll her eyes as he stood to hug Etan.

"How long before they figure out they can't spend their money anywhere?" Etan said before Alex stopped his words with a kiss.

"Such an embarrassment of riches," Alex said. "Looks like Caela's caught on already."

Caela didn't move from her chair beside the window as Alex walked over, a book open on her lap.

"Let me see, sweetheart."

She pursed her mouth for a second, then flashed her three missing teeth.

"No such fing as a toof fairy," she said, her temporary sweet lisp forcing Alex to hide his grin.

"I didn't believe in that stuff either," he said. "But we won't tell the little ones just yet."

Alex leaned down to pick her up without thinking, and her arms went around his neck in a flash. When he stood, he sucked air through his teeth at the first twinge he'd felt for several weeks.

"Alex?" Etan said. "Be *careful*, Caela!"

She twisted in his arms, and Alex's efforts to keep from dropping her drove the pain deeper beneath his ribs.

"No, no!" she cried, tears filling her blue eyes. "Didn't mean to hurt you!"

The rumble of voices and activity behind Alex stopped, and he knew what he'd see before he turned. Etan and the younger children were all watching him, their eyes equally wide and frightened.

Alex turned his head away from Caela, trying to hide his face. The pattern of fear and avoidance was clear and painful all around him. Making love with Etan a few times softened the edges between them, but not nearly enough. And not at all with their children.

Now was the time to break it.

"Listen to me, Caela," he said. "All of you. I'm not hurt anymore, and I'm not sick. It's time you all stopped treating me like I am."

Everyone but Etan and Caela stared for several seconds, then seemed to understand what he was saying. Or they were more easily distracted by the marbles.

Alex was more worried about the two of them.

"I'm not going to bite you, either," he said. He sat on the couch with Caela, pleased that moving more carefully kept the pain at bay. "I've got news for you two anyway."

Etan sat beside them, his face too carefully neutral.

"That's the first time anything has hurt for a while, E. If it does sometimes, but less often, that means I'm getting stronger. Not weaker. I'm strong enough to pick you up now, Caela. Understand?"

"I guess," she said. "I'm the oldest, so I guess you can pick all of us up."

"Maybe not all at once, but that's good enough for me. Etan?"

"That was my fault," he said, squeezing Caela's arm. "You didn't do anything wrong. We can both do better if we help each other remember, okay?"

She glanced at Alex, her face serious, then she grinned at Etan. All of their kids turned to Etan more than before. That made Alex a tiny bit more happy than sad.

"Okay, Daddy E. We'll remember together."

"What's your big news, sweetie?" Etan said. He moved closer to Alex, head on his shoulder. Caela scooted until her legs were across both their laps.

"Everyone's Dreaming of training now. In general like we've been doing when they turn nine, but especially for the Dreamers and Witnesses. It feels like we can cover the basics while they're young, like this hellion. Then as they sort themselves out, we'll work out the specialized classes."

"I get to go to *Dreamer* school?" Caela said.

"Maybe," Etan said. "Depends on what happens when you grow up. You might be a Witness just like Alex and Gena."

"You get to go to school either way," Alex said. "No one feels like we should be delaying until they're older, not anymore. You'll be going with the older kids every morning instead of with your brothers and sisters. That okay with you?"

"Yeah! Will you be teaching us?"

"We both probably will, and Iris and Gena," Alex said. "A lot more when you get older. We'll all figure it out together. You're the oldest born here, and Daddy E didn't start Dreaming until he was eleven. Same with Mom Iris. So we've got at least five years before we have to worry about you starting."

Barely two years later, they all understood how quickly things were changing.

Chapter 31

ETAN GOT out of bed slowly, doing his best not to wake Alex. All of
the Witnesses seemed to sleep lightly, but he had to try. The fear of
his husband getting too run down and getting sick again never quite
left him.

He was rarely awake first, and the children seemed aware of that
fact. Testing his ability to keep up with them and keep them quiet
left him wondering if they did the same to Alex.

Caela answered him before he asked.

"They're *always* like that, Daddy E," she said, shaking her head.

At eight, Caela was fully aware of being the oldest of all of them.
She didn't take *too* much advantage of her status, but she didn't feel
like one of the babies, either.

"Are you feeling okay, Caela?" Etan said. She was pale and more
quiet than usual. He touched her forehead like he still sometimes did
Alex's. She reacted in exactly the same way, drawing back and
scowling.

"I'm *not* sick and I *don't* have a fever. I had a bad dream again, I
think."

Etan stared at her, his stomach a mass of swirling knots. She was
too young for the Dreams, wasn't she? She had to be. Nightmares

were one thing. He'd thought hers had finally stopped two years after she'd seen what happened to Connor and Alex.

"You think? Do you remember your dreams, Caela?"

She shrugged and shook her head. Such a perfect imitation of Alex that Etan couldn't help but smile.

"Sometimes. I think Daddy A remembers them for me."

"Has he been talking to you about your dreams?"

"I think he does at night, when I have the bad ones. The ones I can't remember."

"Okay. Maybe we can both talk to him about it when he wakes up."

Alex still wasn't up by the time Etan got everyone settled down and out to their morning playtime outside and sent Caela off to school. The courtyard behind the apartment building was a perfect setting to keep so many young children occupied and keep parents still concerned about another attack from worrying too much. The new security patrols helped even more. The group playtime was also a perfect way to keep teenagers involved and out of trouble.

Etan sat on the bed beside Alex, watching him breathe. Everything sounded normal, not the rattling strain of when he'd fought off pneumonia. Still, he slept too hard for so late in the morning.

Helping Caela with her bad dreams could explain it.

So could getting sick again.

Etan leaned down and kissed his cheek. Cool, not feverish. And not scowling. Alex smiled, stretching before he pulled Etan down into a hug.

"What's got you up so early?"

"I'm not up early, sweetie. You slept in."

"How much?" Alex said, sitting up on the edge of the bed. "I don't hear stampeding feet."

"They already stampeded downstairs. Caela reassured me they do their best to overrun your authority every morning, too."

Alex blinked. Etan knew he didn't mind getting up with their kids most mornings. Watching the way they all rumbled and laughed together made it clear Alex loved every second.

"I slept through the morning rampage? I'm sorry, E. They're a handful at the best of times."

"No, don't worry. You must have needed it. Come on, breakfast is ready."

"I could get used to this."

Etan waited until Alex ate a reassuring amount before bringing up the Dreams. He usually lost his appetite early on when he wasn't feeling well.

"Caela informs me you've been remembering her Dreams for her."

Alex sighed and closed his eyes for a second.

"For a few weeks now, yeah. I hoped it was normal bad dreams for a while, but I think it's more."

"She's only eight," Etan said. The thought of their daughter having the Dreams at all was bad enough after what'd he'd gone through as an early teenager. And the much worse his grandmother had suffered. "She's still a *baby*."

"I know. She Dreams too early, and they're so damn strong. The strangest thing is she seems to be on the same cycle you are. About the time you start to fall back asleep, she's right in the middle of it."

"The same Dreams?"

"A lot of the time they seem to be. She's not good at describing them yet, but they sound the same. That part *does* worry me. The other adults don't have the same Dreams when you do, E. Not for a while after yours start."

Etan took Alex's hand, the worry forming a harder knot in his belly.

"I don't want her to go through this," he said. "Not so early at the very least. It was hard enough on me at eleven, and I had my father and grandmother to explain what was going on."

"She has us. She's never known a world where the Dreams weren't normal, Etan. Where the Dreams weren't good. She's been learning about it in school for almost two years now. She wants to be just like you, anyway. That's all she ever talks about."

"Like me?" Etan said with a broad smile. "Oh come on. She's your clone, Alex."

"That's probably *why* she wants to be like you. Defying the natural order or something like that. I think she's doing fine. We'll just have to help her as much as we can."

"What if this is too strong in her?" Etan said. "We've never seen the children of Dreamers and Witnesses. I'm afraid it will be like it was for my grandmother, even if we help her."

Alex pushed his chair back, stretching his legs under the table.

"All we can do is pay attention and talk to her. That's what I've been trying to do, make sure she's not so scared in the middle of the night."

"That's not making me feel better. You have to sleep some time. If you get too tired—"

"I'm *fine*, Etan," Alex said, the scowl making an appearance. "I can't just sit by and let her be that afraid and ignore it. I won't. Like you said, she's just a baby."

Etan looked out the window, breathing out hard through pursed lips. The three years since the attack hadn't altered his opinion that Alex was a far worse patient than their children. He knew it for a fact now.

Just as well as he knew his own escalating fears could easily push him into a black hole he was afraid he'd never climb out of.

"Well, I'm not going to sit by and pretend I'm not worried about the two of you. If we're both Dreaming now, we'll have to make some changes. There are four more not far behind Caela who'll probably need just as much attention when *you* need to sleep. If nothing else, staying awake half the night at almost forty isn't the same as when you were twenty-two."

Alex laughed under his breath.

"I was feeling that difference before Sandy relieved me of my spleen. Very much so, and that was only with you. I've already thought about the rest of them coming along. Even I'll admit trying to calm down six Dreamers in one family would be too much for me. Think we'll get lucky and half will be Witnesses?"

"That's a damn good question," Etan said. "We're right in the middle of a giant experiment with no way to figure too many of these things out. Maybe we can talk to Sandy about that, see what she thinks of how the inheritance will go. We probably need to understand more about that going forward no matter what. That doesn't solve the problem of you not getting enough sleep, Alex."

"Well, I have an idea about that, too. I don't much like it, and you won't either. But I'm not sure what else to do with the living arrangements we have here."

Etan looked around their apartment. The big living room beyond the kitchen, cluttered with books and toys and every other evidence of life with kids. The space that felt so huge and decadent when they moved in, especially compared to their cozy shoebox in Chicago, had gotten crowded in a hurry as children joined their family.

"I think joining up two apartments when more houses are ready makes a hell of a lot of sense," Etan said. "Much as I love my grand-parents' place, I think we should stay here."

"Yeah, I do too. I'm talking about here. What if we set up a bed in our bedroom, a small one for whichever kid is starting to Dream?"

"We're already jammed into the smallest room in the place. I'm not quite ready to give up all my privacy with you."

"Neither am I."

Alex smiled with the same warmth in his eyes that made Etan weak in the knees the first time they met. Even with all the changes and trouble and struggle, not to mention five children, that response hadn't faded a bit in all those years.

"We don't have to stay in the smallest bedroom, especially if we do this," Alex said. "And I don't mean they sleep in there all the time, either. From talking to you and other Dreamers, it seems to hit really hard for the first several months. Maybe a year. Then it settles down a bit. Sound right to you?"

"Yeah, I think so. I didn't remember mine back then, either. And I didn't have you to notice things like that."

"How things worked for you and Iris and the others doesn't matter that much, not anymore. We're on the front lines with Caela. She's the first I know of to start Dreaming so young. Maybe she'll settle down sooner. Or at least be able to come wake me when she needs me instead of getting so scared. I need to figure out some way to teach her to know when she's Dreaming, to find me and ask for help. If you're on the same cycle like it seems, I'll be awake anyway."

"The best thing would be a small room close to ours," Etan said. "That might work when we have more space. You're right, we should talk to Sandy. She'll know a lot more about how inheritance works, or at least which of her books to look in. Everything we learn with Caela will make it easier for the younger ones."

"And the ones on the way. It means a lot more sleepless nights, but I'm looking forward to meeting the new babies."

Etan took Alex's outstretched hand. The break from newborns made a lot of sense while Alex was recovering, and for all the rest of them to catch their breath. Iris and Gena were raising four of their children as well. With their youngest just turning three, everyone was excited about new little brothers and sisters.

"Everything we learn about all of them will make it easier going forward," Etan said. "We'll have grandchildren to spoil before we know what hit us."

Alex groaned. He stood and pulled Etan into a hug.

"I am *not* ready to think about that. I'm not ready to even imagine letting our kids go."

"Will you ever be, Daddy A?"

"No. Not even a little bit."

PART IV

OLD WAYS PASS AWAY

Chapter 32

Nearly twenty years passing hadn't dulled Etan's love of the bright sunlight in the living room of their apartment. Especially now that he'd finally admitted he needed reading glasses, even for studying Alex's neat handwriting. The warm breeze drifting in through the open window, perfumed with lilacs even four stories up, managed to lift Etan's gloomy mood a little bit.

He took off the metal-framed glasses and rubbed the ache between his eyebrows, trying to get it to ease up enough for him to be able to think. He could feel the ridge there, the muscles underneath his skin taking on a permanent crease that sometimes looked like a chasm to him in the mirror.

He wasn't a kid anymore at forty-two, but surely he was too young to have such sharp evidence of his own anxiety right there on his face.

He opened his eyes and looked at Alex sitting at the ancient and scarred wooden desk against the opposite wall. All the kids used it for study and homework, resulting in a permanent drift of books, paper, and the wood and charcoal pencils they all knew how to make.

Alex had long ago stopped putting away what the teenagers left there when he needed the space, or asking them to keep the desk neat. He unceremoniously shoved it all into one of the boxes he kept beside the desk just for that purpose and let them sort it out.

Alex wasn't quite as ruthless with the drifts and clutter the younger kids managed to produce in their wake. As long as they confined it all in the corners – and out of the path where adult feet might step on a painful edge – the ongoing games continued. Etan agreed that keeping the toys out in the main living area rather than scattered in the bedrooms made life in general and cleaning in particular much easier.

Etan wasn't sure if he was proud or annoyed that Alex looked so much younger than he did. Alex's hair was still red, though not as dark as when they met. He'd found his own reading glasses in the supply they'd hoarded back when they scouted nearby towns for paper, though he didn't need them as often as Etan did.

If the sunlight caught Alex just right, Etan could see smile lines around his eyes and mouth. Right now, with the light behind him, he looked closer to twenty-five than forty-five.

The biggest sign of his age was the gray in his beard, matching the silver highlights Etan remembered from his vision on their wedding day. Etan thought that only made him more handsome.

He wasn't sure the gray taking over the brown in his own thinning hair did the same at all.

"You okay?" Alex said.

"I'm okay. I'm afraid we're going to have a tough time tonight. I can feel it coming."

Alex raised one eyebrow and sighed, then stood up and stretched. He'd grown a little thicker around the middle, but Etan thought he and Alex were the only ones who knew that. It only showed when Alex was naked, along with the pale, twisting scars below his ribs.

"What Dreams do you think I've been looking at just now?" Alex said, stretching out on the battered but still beloved gray couch with his head in Etan's lap.

"Let's see," Etan said, running his fingers through the red curls. "Couldn't be Mary stirring up trouble here, could it? Taking all of us down with her?"

Alex laughed, shaking his head, then put his hand on the back of Etan's neck. Etan leaned down to meet him in a kiss.

"Of course it is. Do you remember what's going to happen yet? Or when?"

"No, not yet. I can never decide if I envy Iris that or not. Just dreading something doesn't help a damn thing, but I'm not sure remembering it sooner would either."

"Have you asked her about it? Or Gena?"

Etan shook his head, rotating his neck to try to loosen his shoulders.

"They're too wrapped up with the baby coming. If either of them felt something really strong, they would have told us."

"Think this will be the last one?" Alex said, rubbing the back of Etan's neck.

Etan smiled, thrilled all over again at meeting one of their children for the first time. Gena was carrying this one, and with her blond hair and fair skin, they might not have any idea who the father was. Not that it mattered.

Caela, their first child with Iris, was now a fiery-haired teenager with a temper to match. But Etan loved her every bit as much as the brown-haired, studious little boy who'd come next, and all the others. Every one, whether they lived with them or one floor down with Iris and Gena, belonged to all of them.

"Maybe," Etan said. "Iris is thirty-eight this year, Gena's what, forty-one? I kind of hope not, but we're already more lucky than most. They might be getting tired of being pregnant."

"We do have the easy part," Alex said. "At least for the first nine months."

He sat up and moved to the end of the couch.

"Come here. You feel like a bunch of steel cables."

Etan leaned against him, groaning when Alex dug his fingers into his shoulders.

"You keep all your stress right here, don't you?"

Etan tried not to scowl and failed miserably. "Everything I don't keep on my face."

"I love your face, you jackass."

Etan turned toward him, and Alex's lips unerringly found the spot just above his nose, the exact place Etan was most self-conscious about.

"Listen, Alex, I know you Witness-types like to keep your records to yourselves, but has anyone else had this Dream? About Mary?"

"No. I keep hoping someone else will. We haven't had to do anything like this yet."

"You mean stopping her from causing trouble?" Etan said. "We already got her off the Council."

Alex sighed. "That wasn't so bad, just a lot of arguing. It might have made the whole situation worse though. She brings more and more of her followers to every open meeting we have. It's like a fungus. I'm afraid it's all going to play out just like your Dream. I don't think we'll be able to stop them."

Neither of them spoke for a few minutes. Etan was happy to let him work out the knots in his muscles. He hoped Alex wouldn't bring the Dream up again, but he knew his husband too well to expect that.

"I don't see any way around this," Alex finally said. "She *is* going to cause some kind of trouble. And cause a lot of damage for the rest of us while she's at it."

"Unless we're willing to lock them up or get rid of them somehow, yeah. Trouble we might not be able to recover from."

Alex ran both hands down Etan's chest, pulling him closer. He kissed Etan's neck just below his ear.

"No wonder you're so tense. I'm sorry, sweetie. I'm glad you can't remember the Dream."

"Living it's going to be bad enough."

Chapter 33

ETAN WATCHED Caela walking ahead of them toward the Town Hall, her long red curls shifting across her back as she talked to her friends. They walked so naturally in the middle of the street, without even a trace of the need to look both ways. These days a moving vehicle in Wolf Branch or probably anywhere else in North America was rare enough that everyone stopped to watch.

The roads in town were in remarkably good shape over two decades after the last repaving crew passed by. Sort of faded, a bit cracked. Threatening to form a pothole or two in the lowest spots. Etan tried not to think too much about how the roads far to the north where Alex grew up must look.

No one Caela's age or younger would ever have seen an airplane overhead, much less the crisscrossing lines of vapor trails against a blue sky.

She and several of the oldest children had been going with them to Council meetings for months now. Learning the routines and rituals made sense for the next generation of Witnesses and Dreamers. So did letting them learn patience by sitting quietly and listening no matter how much the adults droned on and on.

He had to at least try to stop their daughter from being in the middle of whatever was going to happen now.

"I don't think Caela should be there tonight."

"I tried stopping her earlier," Alex said. "She made it clear if I wouldn't tell her *why* not, she'd bloody well go whether I *want* her to or not."

"That's pretty much what she told me. I guess she has a point. She's been going for almost a year now. I just don't want her in the middle of this mess."

Alex had been helping Caela with the same kinds of Dreams as Etan's since she was eight, and all of her training and education had been geared toward developing that, and dealing with it. At fifteen, she was nearly ready to be on the Council herself.

The time when either of them could say "because I said so" about this or much of anything else was far in the past.

"I was afraid she'd Dream about it, or remember it," Alex said, then he smiled. "She's too damn much like her mother."

"If she Dreamed or remembered, she hasn't told me. That doesn't mean anything though."

"Are you sure it's going to be tonight, E?"

Etan stepped off to the side and stopped, and Alex stopped with him. They were within sight of the red brick town hall, but no one else on the street was paying any attention to them.

"I *feel* it. Don't you? This hasn't lightened up all day."

Alex gave a half-hearted shrug, then he looked out at the people walking past them. Everyone older than Caela was walking slowly, quietly, most of them looking at the ground.

All of them clearly caught up in the dread he could almost see floating in the air, between the brick buildings and through the garden and orchard spaces scattered throughout town.

"I think everyone feels it," Etan said "Everyone who remembers the end, anyway."

"No one her age could know what it means. Not really. Not in their bones the way we do."

"What are we walking into?" a low voice said from right behind Alex.

Iris, Gena beside her. The four of them stood together and watched the nearly silent procession.

"I thought you were staying in," Etan said, his hand on Gena's shoulder.

"I wanted her to, but she never listens to me when I'm awake," Iris said, trying her best to look angry. Gena was rosy and healthy, and well into her ninth month of pregnancy.

"Look around you," she said. "I'm as worried about whatever's happening as everyone else is." She turned to Etan, and he dreaded her question. "Do you know what's going to happen?"

"I haven't had any Memories. Have you, Iris?"

"You don't need to have the Memory," she said, her eyes narrowed. "You had the Dream."

"Is it Mary?" Gena said, looking at Alex. "The trouble she's going to cause?"

That was something many of the Witnesses seemed to share, the ability to hone in on what was coming, even if they didn't foresee it themselves. Etan had seen it happen too many times to doubt it.

"That's the one I've been drawn to," Alex said, taking Etan's hand again.

A few people stood outside the doors of the town hall, but other than that the street was empty. Everyone would be waiting for the four of them.

Between Etan's Dreams and Iris's Memories, they were always in the middle of difficult choices for their community whether they wanted to be or not.

"Can we do anything to stop them?" Iris said.

"I don't think so," Etan said. "We couldn't even stop Caela from being here."

"Where was she going to learn respect for authority?" Gena said, smiling at the three of them. "Not from any of her parents."

He and Alex followed the two women into the conference room. Everyone was already gathered around the long tables set up in a square, Caela with several young people sitting in chairs behind them. Even with such a large crowd – nearly thirty on the Council now – four chairs together remained empty. No one wanted to try to take over leadership on such a difficult night.

As soon as they sat, George Light got to his feet. His curly hair was nearly all white now, but his dark face was nearly unlined. His rich voice hadn't aged one day.

"Welcome brothers and sisters, I hope this day finds you healthy and well. We only have a few things to take care of before we get to new business and new Dreams."

Etan tried to let his mind wander, to let the meeting wash over him as he'd done for so many years. That wasn't working this time. The dread grew within him, taking over all of his body's usual functions and sensations. It wasn't so much what was going to happen, though that was bad enough. Far worse was knowing he couldn't stop it no matter what he did.

Harry Mullins raised his voice, calling Etan's mind back into the room yet again.

"What I'm *saying* is we can't keep letting this go on. We're not talking about one lone scrawny woman anymore. She's stirring up shit with more than enough people to cause us real damage here."

"What exactly do you expect us to do, Harry?" Dana Chen said. "Just randomly round people up and hope we get the right ones?"

Etan turned to Dana, still the trusted leader of their security force. Her gleaming black hair showed a few streaks of silver, probably earlier than it would have if she hadn't taken on such a difficult job. But she showed no signs of wanting to step down.

A few people still weren't quite comfortable with the idea of any kind of organized protection, and that was one of the main things Mary used to cause unrest. Most of the residents of Wolf Branch seemed grateful.

Etan had never quite gotten comfortable with their gratitude.

"It won't have to be random, Dana, not at all," Harry said. "I know exactly who's working with Mary on this."

"How can you possibly know that?"

Etan didn't notice who spoke then, he was too busy watching Harry. The older man *did* know. That was the first thing Etan hadn't doubted throughout this whole awful day. His vision shifted, and he could have answered the question before Harry did.

"I recognize them, all of them. It started about a week ago. I can see it on their faces. Well, in *front* of their faces, more like. Something about their eyes – a cloud, maybe. They all look like Mary's eyes."

Etan watched everyone around the table, waiting to see the recognition. About half of them were scowled or shook their heads. Everyone else, though, either looked surprised or nodded.

He and Harry weren't the only ones.

"How long have you been able to see things like that?" Dana said.

"Oh, I always did," Harry said, his ears turning red. "That was one way I decided who to hire before everything went to hell. Who to invest with. There wasn't any secret research to it. That was how I knew who to fire, too."

"I understand, I can back that up," George said. "I saw something like that in my own congregation days. Has anyone else seen or felt this about people besides Mary?"

The same people Etan had noticed now held up their hands. Dana was unfortunately not among them. She took a deep breath, leaning back in her chair and crossing her arms.

"Even if this were reasonable, and even if every last one of you agrees on who they are, you still haven't said what I'm supposed to *do* about it. Even if I had enough officers to round up a bunch of people, which I don't, where would I put them? We don't exactly have a super max prison right next door."

"We don't need a prison," Harry said, a satisfied look on his face. "We just need them out of here. I was thinking we could ask Mary to be the leader of our next group of settlers. They'd be, what, lucky number nine or whatever such nonsense you want to call it. We can send their discontented asses out to find their own little paradise."

"Dad."

The repeated whisper finally broke through, and Etan looked over his shoulder at Caela. He turned his whole body when he saw her. Her blue eyes were wide and tears were streaming down her face.

"What's wrong?"

"Stop them," she said, loud enough that Alex turned around too. "You've got to *stop* this."

Chapter 34

ETAN CLOSED HIS EYES, his heart nearly bursting inside of him. He hadn't seen this moment coming, not the way their daughter surely had, but he knew this was why the dread was so awful.

This was what he couldn't stop.

Their little girl knowing so many people were going to die, knowing her fathers weren't going to be able to do anything about it. Facing the news of such a terrible loss would be nothing compared to facing Caela right now.

"No, sweetheart, it's going to be okay," he whispered, Alex nodding beside him.

"Don't *lie* to me!"

Her sobbing gasp was loud enough for everyone on their side of the room to look around. Protocol and pretense didn't matter anymore, and neither did people considering Caela to be an adult before she was ready.

Etan pushed his chair back and stood, and a beat later Alex did the same.

"Excuse us," Alex said, his voice rough.

Iris touched Etan's hand, and he leaned down to whisper in her ear. "I think she knows what's coming. We'll get her out of here."

Iris nodded, then turned to Gena.

"Come on," Alex said under his breath, holding out his hands. "Let's go outside for a while."

Caela's lovely face crumpled, and for a second Etan was certain she'd start crying louder. She opened her eyes and nodded, letting Alex pull her to her feet. The three of them walked into the small break room next door and sat together on the blue sofa. The same comfortable chairs and soft lighting, and the TV on the wall that hadn't been used in nearly two decades. Etan glanced over their daughter's head at Alex.

He knew his husband remembered sitting in the same room together almost twenty years ago, Etan finally agreeing to talk to the Council but still scared to death.

Long before they could have imagined such a beautiful creature in their lives.

"They're going to come back if they leave that way," she said, her tears falling again. "Come back and attack us. You have to go back in there and stop them!"

Etan blinked, drawing back.

Attack them? As far as he knew, no one had seen such a thing. He certainly hadn't.

"What did you see, Caela?" Alex said. "Did you have a Memory, like Iris does sometimes?"

Etan didn't want to say it or even think it, but his grandmother Anne often saw Memories, the waking Dreams of remembering things that hadn't happened yet. She'd suffered horribly because of that.

If Caela was having the same, he could only hope she inherited enough of Iris's stability to counteract Anne's struggles.

Caela took a few deep breaths, trying to stop the tears, then gave up.

"I know they'll cause trouble if they stay, I *know* that. I feel that too. But if they leave, they'll come back in a few months, maybe a year. They'll attack us, and security won't be able to stop them. They'll steal enough food and kill enough people that... We won't survive."

"You just saw that?" Alex said, every inch the Witness, even with his own daughter. "It feels solid and real, like we talked about? Not like a daydream?"

"Yes, it's real! It's every bit as real as Mary staying here and causing so much trouble that we don't survive that either. They *can't* stay, and they *can't* go. Have other people seen her causing trouble here if she stays?"

Alex nodded, brushing her hair back.

"Etan had that Dream, and Iris and many others have seen it too."

"But what are we supposed to *do*? Why do we have these goddamn Dreams if we can't do anything to stop this? If we're all going to die anyway, what the hell was the point?"

Etan's heart shattered at the terrible sound in their daughter's voice.

He hugged her, and he felt Alex's arms go around both of them. Their daughter's sobs were tearing him apart. Alex's grip on his shoulder told Etan he wasn't faring any better.

"I've been asking that question since I was eleven years old, sweetheart," Etan said. "Lots of times we can help, make a real difference. But I don't know why this kind of thing happens. I hate it too."

"*Fucking* Mary," Caela said, and the disgust in her voice made Etan wince. "If she'd never been here, none of this would happen."

"Maybe," Alex said, sitting back and wiping her tears. "But there could be some reason we don't know. Maybe if Mary had never been here, things would be even worse. Maybe even if we could stop things like this, that would be the *worst* thing we could do."

Caela scowled and shook her head, and tears filled Etan's eyes again. She was so much like Alex, almost as if Iris hadn't been involved in her making at all. Looking at their daughter, he couldn't imagine he'd thought he wouldn't love children who weren't a genetic mix of their fathers.

His love for her was so fierce partly because he saw Alex so clearly in her.

"Yeah, they keep telling us that in training," she said, brushing at her cheeks. "Hearing the words isn't the same as watching it happen, you know?"

"I know," Etan said. "Listen, you don't have to go back in. One of us can walk you back home, or you can wait out here. Alex and I can tell them what you've seen. There's no reason for you to go through this, love."

Caela rolled her eyes, then looked up at him under her eyebrows. That was a flash of Iris so clear Etan couldn't ignore it.

Of course she wouldn't take the easy way. The more either of them or anyone else suggested it, the more she'd resist.

"I'm the one who's seen it," she said, then took a shuddering breath. "I've never had a Memory this clear before. I feel like… I think I need to see it through or something. Do you understand?"

"I wish I didn't understand quite so well," Alex said, laughing under his breath. "I think both of us do."

"We do," Etan said, half-smiling at his husband. "Ready to go back in? It's fine if you need a little while longer."

Caela looked at the door, and the very air shifted around her. Etan saw it as clearly as ripples in water. Their daughter had come to some kind of decision, some kind of choice that was going to impact all of them far more than even the terrible Memory she'd just seen.

Etan had the strongest urge to pick her up and run. Pick her up just like the day she was born, when she wasn't any longer than his forearm. Just grab her and Alex and all of their children and get the hell away from here, away from this horrifying, empty world they'd been born into.

The remains of humanity would have to learn how to survive without them.

Without his family.

"They're not going to listen to some kid without their strongest Dreamer to back me up, are they?" Caela said. "Or their strongest Witness to those Dreams."

Before either of her fathers could answer, Caela stood, squared her shoulders, and walked toward the conference room.

All they could do was follow.

"She's never going to stop walking away from us, is she?" Alex said, reaching for Etan's hand.

"I just hope she looks back now and then."

By the time they opened the doors, Caela waited beside their empty seats, another chair pulled up behind her. Everyone else around the tables was moving closer together. She moved her chair into the space. When they were settled, Alex and Etan on either side of her, everyone looked at Harry.

"How are we going to get all of them to agree to leave?" Dana said.

Before Harry could answer, Alex stood, his hand on Caela's shoulder.

"Caela has seen a Memory she needs to share," he said. "A Memory about Mary and the others leaving."

Harry looked at them, his eyes narrow. He wasn't used to being interrupted, and he clearly didn't appreciate it.

"Your daughter is not a member of this Council, Alex."

"No, not yet. But only because of her age. She's been having the Dreams since she was eight years old. I'm not the only Witness to verify her Dreams. She knows what's at stake, and she knows when her Dreams and Memories are true as well as any of you do."

Harry pursed his lips, but he waved his hand and sat back. He had more than one child in the same training group as Caela. He couldn't deny her abilities without calling all of the other young people into question.

Alex looked down at Caela and nodded.

She turned to Etan, her eyes wide but no longer crying, then got to her feet. Etan stood beside his daughter and his husband.

"If they leave," Caela said in a weak voice, then she went on more clearly. "If Mary and the others leave, they'll return and attack us. Worse than the raiders from Maple Ridge who killed my grandfather. Worse than the attack that almost killed my father. They'll steal our supplies and kill many of us before we can defend ourselves. We won't… We won't survive long after the attack."

No one moved for several seconds, and Etan would have sworn

he was in a room full of mannequins. He felt the change before he heard sighs all around him.

The Memory had opened up for everyone else at Caela's words, Dana among them this time. She covered her face with one hand. Harry was pale, and George had tears in his eyes. Iris squeezed Etan's hand.

"Many of us have now seen the same Memory," George said in a low voice. "Etan, do you still see the trouble Mary and the other will cause if they stay?"

Before he could answer, Iris stood beside him.

"I've had this Dream as well, I and many others. It hasn't shifted for me, even with Caela's Memory."

Several people around the long tables nodded.

"So both paths lead to our damnation," George said, his tears spilling over.

No one spoke, and after a moment, Alex, Etan, and Iris sat down.

Caela remained standing.

"I believe I know another way," she said, and her quiet voice carried throughout the silent room.

Etan looked at Alex, but only he shrugged and shook his head.

"Your Memory has come to many of us, just like so many of your parents' Dreams have," George said, wiping his face. "Please tell us what you see, Caela."

"We know they can't stay here without causing trouble. And if they leave, they'll return and attack us." She took a deep breath. "We have to make sure they can *never* return."

Etan's mind reeled, trying to imagine what she was talking about. Then his eyes met Alex's, and he knew.

Too late to stop their daughter, too late to stop any of it.

He *knew*.

"My father Etan has had… He had a Dream of Laurel Gap, a town high in the mountains. I had the same Dream."

"No, Caela," Etan said. "Not this."

She raised her voice and kept talking.

"Laurel Gap looks safe and prosperous, with wood and game and coal. But the water there is bad. Something was buried there a long time ago. Something to do with the coal."

"I said no!" Etan reached for her hand, but she pulled away. "Why did you tell her, Alex? Why?"

"I didn't tell her a damn thing!" He looked as frightened as Etan felt.

"If they go to this town, they won't return to attack us," Caela said, nearly shouting now. "They won't *ever* return."

Etan stood, grabbing her shoulders and turning her to face him. She looked back without flinching, her face horribly strong, defiant, and beautiful.

"Who told you this?" he said, shaking her. "Where did you hear about this Dream? Was it Alex?"

Alex stood, glaring at Etan, his strong fingers trying to loosen Etan's grip on their daughter's shoulders.

"I said I didn't tell her," Alex said, his voice nearly a growl.

"He *didn't* tell me," Caela said, trying to pull both of their hands away. "I read it in his journal when he was teaching me about my own Dreams!"

Both men let go, leaving her to stand on her own.

"You did what?" Alex said, his voice soft and airy. "You read the journals of your father's Dreams?"

Caela clenched her fists and turned to Alex.

"I didn't read all of them, no. Of *course* not. But a long time ago, when I was first Dreaming, I heard you say I'd had the same as him one night. One I couldn't remember. You didn't write it in my journal, so I read the one in his."

"You shouldn't have done– " Alex started, but Caela cut him off, her face as red as his.

"It was *my* fucking Dream! You shouldn't have kept it from me!"

"Hold on, slow down," Etan said, desperate to stop the shouting in front of everyone else. "We can talk about this more at home. Was it the Dream about that town, Alex? Laurel Gap?"

Alex scowled, shaking his head. Etan knew he wasn't denying the Dream. He didn't want to acknowledge what it meant.

"Come on. Was it?"

"It was the same Dream," Alex said, looking down. "The town with the bad water."

Etan closed his eyes, cold nausea working through his whole body. He would have given almost anything if he could step backwards in time, just a few minutes. If he could be the one to bring up the necessary, terrible course they had to take.

If he could save their little girl from having to do such an awful thing before she was grown enough to even think about it.

"Alex, can you confirm you have Witnessed two Dreamers having this Dream?" George Light said, his deep voice as soothing as his words were damning. "I remember you sharing Etan's Dream several years ago."

"I confirm it," Alex said, his face strained and pale now. "Both Etan and Caela have had this Dream."

All three of them finally sat. Etan wondered if the other two had lost all strength in their legs as badly as he had.

"I know this is a difficult thing," Harry Mullins said, his voice as compassionate as the night Alex nearly died. "But Caela gives us a solution that sounds true to me. It *feels* true."

Etan clenched his jaw, trying to keep the nausea from getting worse. He'd made the terrible choice to end a human life when the drifter attacked Connor and wounded Alex nine years earlier.

None of that changed Etan's fundamental belief. With so dreadfully few people still living – only a few thousand outside of Wolf Branch that he knew of, with solid rumors of more farther away – sending any of them to death was almost the worst sin he could imagine.

The only worse sin was their daughter being the one to set it into motion.

"It feels true to me as well," Iris said.

Etan didn't have to look at her to know she was crying. He heard it in her voice.

"And to me," Dana Chen said, wiping at her own eyes.

One by one, everyone around the table either spoke or nodded. Not one person disagreed. When only Etan and Alex were left, they looked into each other's eyes. They joined hands behind their daughter without saying a word.

"We still haven't figured out…" Dana said, then she took a deep breath and shook her head sharply. "We don't have a way to get them all to leave."

"The idea I had before was a lottery," Harry said, looking at his hands clasped on the table. "A chance to leave and start fresh, for people besides the new settlers. We'd just have to rig the results. Simple as that."

Etan's nausea was only getting worse, but he knew even going outside and throwing up wouldn't make it go away. He had to say something. He had to try to stop this.

Even if it did lead to the end of all of them, he couldn't let Caela be responsible for murder.

"It's *not* simple, not one goddamn bit," he said through a tight throat. "We'll be choosing a bunch of people, when there are hardly any left, and sending them off to die. We'll be their judge, jury, and executioners."

"We're not choosing them," Gena said, reaching past Iris to touch his arm. "They're planning to hurt the rest of us, whether they stay or leave. It was *their* choice. We have to think about the bigger picture here."

"Fuck the bigger picture!" Etan said, trying not to wail like Caela had earlier. "This is too much, certainly too much for a fifteen year old girl!"

"No, Etan, no," Alex said. "Look at me."

Etan squeezed his eyes shut for a second, not wanting to hear what his husband had to say. For that one second, for the first time since he was barely older than Caela, he didn't care about *anything* Alex had to say.

He didn't care if every single person on the planet died either. He couldn't stand such damage to his own family.

He finally looked into Alex's eyes: the saddest, and the oldest, he'd ever seen them.

"I don't like this any more than you do, but she's not a child anymore. This was the Memory of an adult, and she made the choice of an adult. Her Dream was the same as yours. You both had it for a reason."

Alex looked at Caela for a second, then squeezed Etan's hand.

"Can't you feel it, E? Everything changed. We have a chance now. We all do."

Etan squeezed back, the nausea shifting to a deep ache inside of him. He did feel the difference, the lifting of the dread and the dead end they'd all been facing.

Caela had put their solution together when he hadn't been able, or willing.

She'd spoken it aloud and shown them the way.

Salvation or not, his whole body twisted in agony over what she'd done.

He and Alex moved their arms up to their daughter's shoulders. She didn't say a word, but she leaned into their support.

"We'll have to be so careful," Dana said. "The biggest danger is anyone else finding out what we've done here."

"No, that's not the biggest danger," Etan said. "Not even close. The biggest danger is we all have to live with it."

Chapter 35

ALEX DRUMMING his fingers on the ancient wooden desk was the only sound in the quiet apartment. He was careful to tap with the pads of his fingers rather than the nails to keep it that way, though he wasn't quite sure why.

The scarred and worn surface had stayed miraculously clear of clutter and toys and papers for days now. Alex was surprised to wish for a mess he could either grumble over or deal with.

Outside the open window, Wolf Branch was unusually still and silent as well. The soft breeze playing over his skin, promising rain later on, explained some of that. But he knew everyone else was preparing for the difficult day when the next group of so-called settlers would leave.

Etan and most of their kids and almost everyone else was out helping today, like they had for the last couple of weeks and would for the next few days.

Learning how to prepare food and belongings for the trip. Getting experience with maintenance on the trucks and ATVs, so everyone could keep them running for as long as possible. Working with Mary and her followers to explain and teach and share what they'd all figured out so far, to send all that knowledge out into a new community so it would thrive.

And Alex and Etan and it seemed like all the residents of Wolf Branch who weren't going with Mary knew all the effort was a cruel charade. A vicious and nasty lie. A sickening play they were all caught up in that would result only in death if they all played their parts well enough.

That wasn't the worst of it, though. Not as far as Alex was concerned.

The worst of it was Caela knew what was coming and how well she'd done *her* part, better than any fifteen-year-old ever should have.

Neither Etan nor Alex had said a word earlier, when Etan headed out with the rest of the kids. Off to learn what they could, sadly including how to put on a good face. They'd all pretended nothing was unusual about both Alex and Caela deciding to stay home.

These preparation days had long been one of Alex's favorite times, with Caela never far from his side. He loved the increasingly rare chance to practice and teach his Engineer Alex skills, to help expand the precarious number of people roaming the empty world. They'd both done their share even this sad time around, up until today.

As soon as he'd opened his eyes that morning, Alex had known without needing one of Etan's Dreams that he and Caela would be sitting this one out.

Maybe he'd had a rare Dream of his own.

More likely he'd known through his own ordinary magic.

He focused on the swirls and textures of the wood under his fingertips, both natural and caused by countless years of use. Darker and lighter wood grain. A scratch here, a stain or a faded water ring there.

All part of the patterns that shaped his life.

The way Caela turned her head away the night before when one of the little ones giggled. The way she twisted her fingers through her lovely red curls. The way she gradually stopped meeting anyone's eyes over the last few days.

That turn in her mood didn't take a genius or a fortune-teller to catch. Only someone who knew her so well, and loved her even more.

But…the play of dust motes through the morning light. The rise and fall of their children's voices over breakfast. Even the beat of Alex's own heart, heavy with worry for Caela.

All those ordinary things let him know she needed him to wait for her, today.

He pretended not to glance at his current stainless steel watch, and anyone else in Wolf Branch wouldn't have had anything to glance at.

Two and a half hours since Etan and the younger kids had headed out, and still not a sound from Caela.

Alex stared out the window at the empty street for a minute, then got up and walked slowly into the kitchen. Whenever she was ready, a cup of warm holly tea with Walt's honey certainly wouldn't hurt. He was busy distracting himself by planning the next maintenance round on the basement boiler – the source for winter heat and precious hot water year-round – when Caela finally spoke from behind him.

"Could you make me a cup, please?"

"Already thought of that, sweetheart. Get us a couple of mugs?"

Alex lifted the strainer full of steaming soaked leaves out of the tea, waiting for it to drain. Despite the somber mood between the two of them, he smiled when he turned and saw what she'd chosen. Both brown and vaguely mug-like, the outer surface covered with unbelievably small fingerprints under the patchy glaze. No handle, but the bottoms were more than thick enough to hold without risking a burn.

Caela's own efforts at pottery when she was first at school. Thankfully the teachers had taken the time to smooth and properly glaze the interiors.

Alex was certain every adult who'd received one of these treasures kept them as carefully as he and Etan did. A row of similar mugs made by each of their children's sweet tiny hands took up the whole top shelf above the sink.

Only Gwen and Eddie enjoyed pottery enough to practice well past that first class. Alex never tired of them bringing something new and beautiful home, nor of using the plates or bowls or cups or flower vases every day.

Caela flashed a quick smile as she added a generous amount of honey to each mug.

"I was quite the artist, huh?"

"Artist enough that we've been happy to use them for ten years."

She stood beside him, staring into her tea as she stirred it.

Perhaps watching the patterns in liquid and steam for herself.

Alex waited.

"None of them know what's coming, do they? Mary and her people, I mean."

"They don't seem to, no," Alex said. "That's probably for the best."

She nodded once, still focused on her mug.

"Do you think they know it was me?"

Her face was calm, but Alex caught the faint tremble in her voice loud and clear.

"I don't think they know anything besides getting to leave on their great adventure."

Caela grunted, leaning her head forward so Alex couldn't see her face through the fiery curtain of her hair.

"It's a grand adventure all right. A one way trip to the grave, courtesy of me. If anyone ever bothers to bury them."

Alex had learned through Caela's tempers and tantrums a few years ago that she might not want a hug from him or anyone else, much as his heart ached at the soft whisper of her crying.

"What kind of person would *do* that?" she whispered. "Tell the whole Council to send a bunch of people off to die. When you *both* tried to stop me."

"The kind of person who knows how important her Dreams are. How to be true to them. Etan had the Dream too, remember?"

"Yeah, I read all about it, didn't I? I'm sorry about that, I really am." Caela tilted her head back now, letting her hair fall out of the way, away from her tear-streaked face. "Dad E didn't get anybody killed, either."

"I'm sorry too, Caela. I shouldn't have kept your Dream from you. You were old enough to know about them for a long time before then. You're old enough now to know how true Etan is to what he Dreams. What he sees. Even when it's hard." Alex paused, waiting for Caela to look up at him. "Even when some might call it murder."

She scowled for a second, then looked down again to take sip of her tea. A clear sign that she wanted to know, but she didn't want to admit it.

"I know you remember the day I was attacked," Alex said. "Much as I wish you didn't. Did anyone ever tell you what happened to the person who did it?"

"The monster. I heard he died. I always wondered if it was the rocks everyone threw at him."

Alex tilted his head to the side.

"*She* did die that day, but not from a rock. Etan had a vision, one of the few times he's had a Memory like you and Iris do, and your great-grandmother Anne did. He saw himself at the jail, giving the monster a choice between poison and a gun. She didn't speak, but she drank the poison. He never needed the gun."

Caela's red-rimmed eyes widened. "So you're saying…"

"All I'm saying is sometimes good people have to do terrible things. *Good* people, Caela. Like Etan. And like you. You might not remember this part, but I was trying to kill her when she stabbed me."

"I do. Because she grabbed Connor."

Alex closed his eyes, nodding. He remembered the fury that boiled out of him that day, the worst he'd ever known. He hoped to never know it again.

"The thing is, I *would* have killed her if she hadn't stopped me," he said. "I would have later if I hadn't been flat on my back."

"That makes sense, though." Caela's brow again furrowed, the same way Alex knew his own did. He saw the evidence of that habit in the mirror every day. "She tried to hurt one of your kids, you know? What I did… I don't think it was the same."

"Wasn't it? You should ask Etan about that sometime. Don't you think he would have told the Council the same thing if he'd had the

Memory before you did? He acted on a Memory at the jail that day when I was in the hospital, and not an easy one."

Caela looked away, but she didn't disagree.

"You knew Mary and everyone with her were going to hurt *all* of us," Alex said. "You understood when none of the rest of us could. You saw the way through. I wish you hadn't been the one to do this, and Etan does, too. But doing the right thing, the hard thing, doesn't make you a bad person."

Caela took a long, deep breath, then finished her tea. She studied Alex's face the same way she had his and Etan's and everyone else's since before she made the precious mugs. Making sure he was telling the truth. Apparently finding what she needed, she leaned closer for a hug.

And Alex found that embrace was what *he* needed, even more than he needed to give it.

Chapter 36

EARLY ON THE day of Mary and her group's departure, Etan couldn't begin to manage the cheerful façade he knew he'd need. His relief that everything had proceeded so smoothly from idea to imminent murder only drove his guilt and despair deeper.

Harry's lottery had gone off without a hitch. Not one "winner" had declined, and no one in Wolf Branch argued about the result. Etan would have sworn people who were neither Dreamer nor Witness had taken on some of those traits as the days passed.

Or maybe it was the gloom and sadness that hovered over everyone, on the Council or not.

After a mostly silent morning, he'd finally taken the excuse to head back into the bedroom by himself. Both he and Alex often caught up on sleep in the afternoon, when they really needed it. Today more than a lack of sleep drove him to escape.

Watching their kids play or study or even argue only reminded him how many children would be heading out later in the day. Heading out to their deaths as surely as they would have later brought death to Wolf Branch, yes. But no less horrible to contemplate.

Etan and Alex had often talked about moving out into one of the larger bedrooms once they didn't need quite so much room for children. For the brief moments when Alex could manage to contemplate that oncoming reality, at least. After so many years, Etan wasn't sure he wanted to leave the cozy space.

They could walk around their bed, but not a whole lot more. Two windows on either side let in plenty of fresh air but no morning or afternoon sunlight. Perfect for such frequently interrupted sleep.

A small bookshelf held all the fiction books either of them wanted to read someday, either from Anne and Evan's collection or from the town library, still lovingly maintained decades after the world's last big fiction publications. A new corner of the library held hand-bound volumes of the heavy fiber and cloth paper everyone learned to make in school now.

The soft green comforter Etan was currently face down on had come from his own childhood bedroom. With his mother's careful mending and his ongoing attempts to learn how himself, he hoped it would outlive him and be passed on to one of their children.

Same for Iris's paintings hanging over the bed and on the opposite wall. She'd somehow managed to capture each of their children, and not with the nearly photographic realism she taught to kids and adults alike at the old school. Impressionistic shapes, colors, hints and suggestions. Even though only Gena usually understood the most stylized and odd of Iris's paintings right away, with Alex close behind her, Etan recognized each of their children at first glance.

Their children.

All the children of Wolf Branch and anywhere else in the empty world were precious.

All *humans* were.

And yet they were sending so many off to die today.

"What have we done?" Etan whispered.

He jumped when Alex spoke from right beside the bed.

"Only what we had to, E," Alex said, stretching out on the bed with his arm around Etan. He smelled of earth and growing things, and his own clean sweat. "Only what we had to."

Etan shook his head, but he curled against his husband.

"At such a cost."

"It isn't going to be easy, "Alex said. "They didn't give us any choice though. We couldn't let them put all of us at risk that way."

Etan raised up to look at Alex, at the circles under his eyes, the deeper lines on his face. He knew he looked older and more weary too.

And Caela seemed to have aged ten years in just a few weeks.

"I hate what she's having to go through," Etan said. "She's too young for any of this."

"I hate what you're going through, too." Alex leaned his forehead against Etan's. "You didn't do this. Neither did Caela. I wish you could *both* stop feeling guilty."

"Do we really have to go to this thing?"

Alex pulled him close again and stroked his hair, as if Etan were one of their children having a particularly moody bad day.

Etan knew he was acting younger than Caela, younger than almost all of their children, but he couldn't stop himself. Watching Mary and her followers walk off to their deaths was worse than the first day of school or going to the doctor, things he'd fought kicking and screaming before the old world ended.

Going to this with a smile on his face felt impossible to him, even with Alex by his side.

"I think George is right," Alex said. "We've seen every group off so far, every single one. If we skip this or send them away in the middle of the night, especially with all the trouble Mary's been in the middle of, it'll cause too much suspicion. We're all going to have to do our best."

"I don't think I can," Etan said, his throat tight and achy. "One look at me and everyone will know."

Alex hummed low and sweet, and Etan wished he could curl up in his lap and go to sleep. He'd often envied their kids that when they were babies, being so warm and safe and secure against Alex's body. He'd give just about anything to be able to do that now.

"Let me tell you a secret," Alex said, his lips close to Etan's ear. "If you marched right up to Mary, to her broken Witnesses and followers and shouted the truth, none of them would hear a word you said. There's something off about the way she Dreams, the way they all do. And the way they *feel* the Dreams. Something spoiled or corrupted, I think. Maybe that's the reason they all have to go, all at once like this."

"Why were they here in the first place though? Caela's right about that part, what was the point? Just to torment all of us and see if we could go through with murder?"

"Who knows? It could be they all needed to be in a group so whatever the problem is wouldn't spread. Did Caela tell you about Mary's children?"

Etan took a deep breath, trying to pull his lover's scent inside his own body, then sat up against the headboard and pillows. Alex moved beside him.

"No, she hasn't mentioned it. Not to me, at least."

"I don't think she talked to anyone but Gena about this," Alex said, a sad half-smile on his face. "We might be too close. Anyway, Mary had three kids in her training group, two boys and a girl. Caela said all three of them seemed to have Dreams, but they got...*lost* in them or something."

"Lost? I don't understand."

"I'm not sure I do either, or anyone else. It sounded like the Dreams were right once in a while, matching with other Dreams, and those felt true to all the Witnesses. But the kids had a hard time telling the Dreams from reality. Caela said it was pretty scary sometimes."

Etan groaned, covering his face. He'd heard both of his grandparents talk about how Anne's own grandmother often got lost in time, lost in what he was sure now were her Memories. Two generations before Anne had them, and two more before Etan and so many others finally started.

She'd ended up basically institutionalized because of her frequent breaks with reality. Etan sometimes wondered how many other early Dreamers or Witnesses had suffered the same or worse, with no way to know their seeming madness would eventually save the remnants of humanity.

"Just one more damn thing Caela's had to deal with over all of this," he said. "She shouldn't have had to see that."

Alex pulled Etan's hands away and held onto them.

"She's a tough kid, E. She's not falling apart. What I'm saying is whatever sort of gift Mary and those with her have, it doesn't seem true. It's too weak or too strong, or maybe it's just broken somehow. The same thing is showing up in all their kids, not just Mary's."

"So we're thinning the herd? Culling them out before they can breed more?"

Alex shrugged. "Yeah, maybe that's exactly it. Our herd is pretty thin now, but that's why they can do so much damage. And you keep forgetting *they're* making this choice, not us. Don't you think it's odd that not one person has complained about not winning the lottery to go with them? And not one of the winners has declined."

"That's the one thing that's getting me through all of this," Etan said. "No one who's staying or going seems to feel anything off about the whole thing. No one outside the Council, anyway."

"Has anyone told you about Mary's Dreams lately?"

Etan raised his eyebrows, waiting to see what he'd have to absorb next. He didn't think he had room for a whole lot more.

"She's been Dreaming about the new place they're going to," Alex said. "How they're going to thrive and be happy and powerful."

"Is anyone buying into that?"

"The Witnesses in her group believe it's true, and so do the other Dreamers. The strange thing is it feels true to Witnesses who *aren't* part of her circle. I felt the same when I heard one of them talking about it. Chilled me to the bone, but it felt as true as one of your Dreams. She's not making these up. It's like she's Dreaming what she needs to for them to go through with this."

Etan blew his breath out through his lips, looking out the window at the green and brown of trees on the hillside.

"I don't know if that reassures me at all, Alex. If it comforts them and makes this go as smoothly as it can, that can only be a good thing. But if these Dreams are true, and the Dreams Caela and I had about all of them dying are true, how can we ever be sure about our Dreams again? We could be Dreaming whatever we want to see at any time."

Alex nodded, and Etan's heart broke as he saw that uncertainty settle onto his face and body. The downturn of his mouth, the lowering of his shoulders and head. He'd last seen Alex fall apart like that when they first talked about the Dreams, long ago and far away in their sweet little shoebox apartment overlooking Lake Michigan.

"Not what you *want* to," Alex said. "I didn't say that. It could be what you *need* to. I wondered about that, too. Since all of this started back in Chicago, I've just accepted your Dreams were true, even when you didn't. I can't think too much about that, honestly. If I start doubting what got us this far, I'll probably lose my mind in a hurry."

Etan shivered, trying to push the guilt away before it could sink in and start gnawing at him. Even if the Dreams had always seemed to be driving him crazy, they somehow kept Alex sane. He wasn't willing to disrupt even that cold comfort.

Alex tilted his head then, squinting.

"The one thing we don't ask, any of us, is where these Dreams come from. We wonder if they're real, if they're true, but not why you have them in the first place. I used to think it was because we were all trying so hard to survive through the next day. That's not nearly as desperate as it used to be, and still, no one asks."

"There might be a reason for that," Etan said, surprised at the instant jump in his heart rate. "If we're all afraid to, that could be something that protects us. The same way we knew we had to head southeast before everyone started dying."

"I know, I guess. I feel that dread sometimes, and that draw. I've always wondered what it is we're following though. Haven't you?"

Etan was shaking his head before he spoke, cold chills running up and down his arms and legs now.

"It's not so much that I haven't wondered. It's more that I'm *afraid* to, you know? This has all been hard enough with some way to know what to do, some kind of guidance."

"Are you afraid the Dreams will stop if we ask too many questions?"

Etan was terribly afraid of losing the Dreams. He and the other Dreamers had felt horribly blind right after the attack that nearly took Alex away. He couldn't explain how he could miss something he rarely remembered, but that didn't make it any less true.

Etan sighed, wanting this conversation to disappear the way the Dreams had then.

"We don't know what made them start, so we can't know what might make them stop. I just don't want to piss off whatever gods are involved here."

Alex smiled, then kissed one of Etan's hands.

"You sound downright religious, my dear."

"Just call it paranoid."

Alex looked at his watch, a relic of their past lives he still refused to give up.

"We need to get down there. I don't want Caela to be in the middle of this without us. She still needs us, no matter what she and everyone else might think."

Etan reluctantly followed his husband downstairs into the courtyard between the buildings, full of flowers and fruit and children. As they had since the horrible day of the attack, the youngest among them gathered outside here in fair weather, in the basement when it was nasty out. At least a few adults stayed with the bunch all the time.

Their kids and several others swarmed around Alex the same way they did anytime he or they came home, as if they hadn't seen each other in a thousand years.

Etan knew their children all loved him, and he adored every one of them. The closeness and trust and silly playfulness he'd gained with them when Alex was so sick remained, but it was never quite the same.

The affection between their children and Alex was as natural as breathing, as joy and laughter. He transformed himself into a six foot tall kid without even trying.

"I fucking hate the idea of giving this up," Alex muttered as they walked away.

One of the many long and painful discussions among Council members since the night Caela shared her Dream – and Etan's – had been about how to train young Dreamers and Witnesses. The talk centered on routines and rituals, ways to prepare their children to pair up as smoothly as possible.

Ideas about separate living arrangements for older children bubbled under the surface, though. Too often.

No one had said a word about Alex doing anything wrong, least of all Etan.

But Etan knew how viciously Alex blamed himself for what Caela had put herself through. Mainly because Etan blamed himself every bit as harshly.

"We don't have to give anything up," Etan said. "Not yet. Maybe not at all."

Alex grunted. "What were we just saying about being a good example?"

Alex was trying to smile, but it only pointed out how hard he was trying not to cry. Etan caught his hand.

"Making sure the Council stands together today is a little different than letting someone else raise our kids, Alex. No one's suggesting that."

"Maybe not from the day they're born, no," Alex said. "We can make sure they feel secure for eight years, maybe eleven. But when they really get into growing up and need us the most, off they go to some kind of boarding school. 'Sorry, kids!'"

"That's *not* going to happen. We're just trying to figure out how to handle their training. That's all."

"Yeah, I know that. I'm the one who fucked up training Caela badly enough that we ended up here."

"Hey," Etan said, slowing down before they got to the crowded square, barely visible between two low brick buildings. "She's not fucked up by any means. She's not even sixteen years old and she saved our asses, remember? That's *not* because she was badly trained."

"I never should have kept that Dream from her. It never should have been her place to save us."

"Well, you didn't make any more mistakes than I did," Etan said, touching Alex's cheek. "You're right. None of us understand how this works. Maybe it *had* to be Caela. What you did was train her to be as strong and tough as she is. I'm damn proud of her, and of you, too."

Alex smiled, a real one, then stepped forward into Etan's arms.

"No one can expect any of us to just make a change this big overnight," Etan said. "Some kind of dorm might be good later on, but not now. That would be too much for everyone. Don't forget every single person wants you to be involved in figuring all of this out. I don't want them out of my sight either. Okay?"

"Okay. I just can't stand the thought of it, letting them go when they're still babies. Letting Caela go in a couple of years is going to tear my guts out."

Chapter 37

WHAT EVERYONE in Wolf Branch called the Square wasn't so much a typical four-sided space as an open, paved area on the far side of town. Etan vaguely remembered a few old, falling-down buildings finally getting demolished when he was a kid. The empty spot turned into a gathering place before anyone could decide what to build there.

Farmers markets, town celebrations for spring, summer, and fall. Birthday parties and family reunions. The town wisely decided to add a few facilities and grass and pavement rather than buildings, and the Square was born.

Maple and dogwood trees grew around the edges, and raised beds in between still held flowers like they had years ago. The addition of mulberry, cherry, and plum trees added color along with a harvest. No one had complained about the addition of strawberry beds and raspberry bushes, either. Or hops vines for a satisfying variety of beers and ales.

The Square still served as a gathering point, most importantly when one of the groups of settlers was ready to depart Wolf Branch and reestablish another human town. Once or twice a year over the past ten, groups who'd straggled in from the outside recovered, gathered their strength, and learned how to survive in the new world.

Then they walked out to one of the roads out of town to do just that.

Mary and her group would indeed be lucky number nine.

The supply of precious vehicles, from four-wheelers to Etan's old van to a couple of big four-wheel drive trucks, would be loaded and waiting, ready to haul supplies and people before locals brought them back.

The crowd gathered today looked about the same as when any of the new colonies had set off in the past, with almost everyone in their community there. A closer look showed Etan and Alex they weren't the only ones who'd decided to leave the younger ones at home.

The youngest were around Caela's age, and Etan didn't see anyone that age who hadn't been at the Council meeting that awful night. Their daughter stood in that group, not far from the rest of the Council.

No one said a word about only adults coming, but apparently no one had to.

"Took you long enough," Caela said, hugging both of them. "It's calm so far. I don't think anyone else knows what's happening."

"I wish *you* didn't," Etan said, getting exactly the rolled eyes he expected from their daughter. "None of Mary's group are here yet?"

Caela shook her head, glancing around the crowd. People were crowded around the edges, under the trees, with a space left open in the middle.

"Nope. They'll be just late enough to keep us all waiting and make some kind of grand entrance. And exit."

"You're in better shape than I am, sweetheart," Etan said, kissing the top of her head.

"No, not really. Just trying to maintain until this is over."

Before Etan could think up a way to try to make her feel better – a way that didn't feel hypocritical – Dana Chen walked up beside him. Her face was composed, but her eyes were red and puffy.

"That was the toughest security meeting I've ever had to lead."

"I'm sorry, Dana," Etan said. "Did they understand?"

"They'll do what I asked them to whether they understand or not."

When Dana glanced around to see who was close by, Alex moved closer and Caela walked away.

"What I didn't tell the whole Council is neither my team nor anyone else will understand how serious this is until the first ones try to come back," she said, tension showing on her face. "That will be bad enough to convince all of them. I didn't try too hard today."

Alex put an arm around the much smaller woman.

"You saw that in your Dream?"

She leaned against him for a few seconds, closing her eyes. When she looked at Etan again, they were more red but she still wasn't crying.

"I did, several times. They're not going to be… By the time they make it back here they'll be pretty far gone. Mentally and physically. Security will take care of itself after that."

Etan touched her shoulder, not sure what to say. This wasn't the first time he was relieved he hardly ever remembered his own Dreams, not by a long shot. He often felt guilty for waking Alex with such horrors after he read his journals the next morning.

"You did the right thing by having your people drive the vehicles and bring them back," Etan finally said. "It's going to be bad enough here already."

The noise level rose at the east end of the Square. The crowd parted like water, and Mary strode into the middle of the empty space. All the other lottery winners, mostly her followers to begin with, filled in the space around her. Everyone shifted until the Council members were gathered in a group, with Mary at the head of her much larger group just a few feet away from Etan.

Neither he nor Alex had ever even pretended they wanted to be in charge, and he knew no one would have told Mary where the Dream of their exile came from.

Somehow she knew to focus on him.

As long as she wasn't looking at Caela, a few feet away with her friends, he would take whatever came.

George Light moved beside Etan and Dana. Etan felt a small

hand slip into his, and he looked down into Gena's green eyes. Her delivery of their beautiful little boy two weeks ago had gone smoothly, but her face showed how tired she was. Iris stood by her side.

"Brothers and sisters," George said, his voice clear and strong. "We're gathered together to celebrate our survival and our strength. We are once again blessed to have enough people to see a group of explorers off and wish them well."

The crowd around them applauded and cheered, and Etan was sure they were all more subdued than usual. The group around him certainly was.

The Council members did well with the illusion of celebration, considering what they were facing.

But they all avoided each others' eyes.

"The journey will be difficult, to be sure," George went on, "but the rewards will be great. We offer you the gift of food so you may prosper in your new home."

George handed Mary a carefully wrapped bundle of seeds and cuttings, well-prepared for the journey.

Everyone on the Council seemed to feel the same way. They hated to waste the plants, especially the ones that didn't require hand-pollination. But just as with this ritual send-off, not giving the plants would have caused far too much suspicion.

Mary took the packet and bowed her head, following the same traditions George was. George held out his upturned hands, giving her the chance to speak. This too was tradition, but so much more risky than sacrificing part of their food supply.

Mary turned slowly, making eye contact with several people in the crowd. When she came back around to the Council members, she moved more slowly. Etan thought she hadn't missed a single person in their smaller group. Before he was ready, it was his turn.

He returned her gaze, hoping he wasn't hurting Alex's or Gena's hand but needing the support. The accusation or fear he was afraid of wasn't in Mary's eyes at all.

He was sure he saw defiance, though, and triumph.

She finally turned away before she spoke.

"We thank you all for your kindness and generosity. We won't forget those who supported and encouraged us as we set out on our journey. The land ahead of us is rich and fertile. We look forward to sharing the bounty we find with each and every one of you."

She turned to Etan again with her last words, and all the hair on his body tried to stand on end. He thought Alex was right, that her gift of Dreaming was broken somehow.

Her visions were closer to insanity.

Even so, that part had sounded like a *prophecy*.

George saved him right before he knew he'd scream with the weight of Mary's gaze.

"Good journey!" George cried, throwing his arms wide.

"Good journey!" everyone in the crowd responded.

The people at the far end of the Square parted, creating a path for the new settlers. No one in Mary's group moved for several seconds while she continued to stare at Etan. Iris stepped forward and took Mary's hand, distracting her at last.

"Good journey, Mary. I wish you luck and prosperity."

Without a word to anyone else or a backward glance, Mary turned and walked through the middle of her followers. Etan let out a breath he felt like he'd been holding for a hundred years as they fell into place behind her.

The number of people Caela's age and even younger hurt his heart, but he was sure the cost would be worth it in the end. He had to believe that if he was going to keep breathing.

"For fuck's sake, are you okay?" Alex said.

He reached up to touch Etan's face, and Etan caught his hand, holding tight, then kissing Alex's palm.

"I am now. I was afraid she was going to cut my heart out before she left and use it for fertilizer."

"I think she was trying to," Gena said.

Harry Mullins walked toward them, his eyes still on the last of the group leaving the Square. He wasn't his normal, confident self. His face looked pale and washed out except for the dark circles like bruises under his eyes.

"You all coming back to the town hall after this?"

Etan's brain chugged for a second, still trying to clear out the afterimage of Mary's burning gaze. The missing piece finally clicked into place when lanky Walt Colley ambled up behind Harry. Despite his own Dreams, Walt had managed the trick of avoiding permanently serving on the Council, although no one ever questioned that he belonged on those occasions he decided to join them.

Especially not when Walt's years of hard work building up the honeybee colonies and teaching others to do the same helped provide the sweetness they so badly needed right now.

Gena spoke up beside Etan.

"I wouldn't miss it. I spent the past few days and all morning pumping enough milk to get the baby through my hangover."

"Think you have enough non-milk beverages for all of us?" Alex said, smiling at Etan.

Etan didn't want to go, not at all. But isolation probably wasn't the best thing after they'd all had to do such a terrible thing as one.

"Well, thanks to science and the printed word," Harry said, "and very generous help from our fellow natives, we've got quite a nice little setup going. It's not far from where the two of you used to live, near Laura and Connor's old place. Might not be the most refined thing you've ever tasted, but it will definitely get the job done. Walt's honey cuts it like a charm."

"That's a real hard thing you had to do just now," Walt said, his words slower than a couple of years ago. "If I can help ease your minds, I'm gonna do just that."

The sound of motors revving up, then heading out of town made the decision easier.

"Count me in," Etan said. "Will the kids be okay?"

All of them turned toward Caela and her friends, still standing together. Their daughter was speaking at that moment, holding hands with another young woman and looking into her eyes.

For at least the thousandth time, Etan was thankful she was so much like Alex.

"We figured they could join us for one drink." George said. "One *watered down* drink. Sandy and Dennis don't drink, so they'll go upstairs and spend the night with our youngest members. The little ones at home will be fine overnight. It's all arranged."

The others turned toward the town hall, and within a few minutes the Square was nearly deserted. Alex put his arm around Etan's waist.

"No one's going to forget, E. No one wants to do this again. But I need to forget for at least a little while."

"Just make sure I make it home at some point. Make sure I'm wherever you are."

Five years would pass before another departure hit Alex or Etan as hard.

PART V

TOWARD THE NEW WORLD

Chapter 38

EVERYTHING in the apartment was in the right place. Dishes clean and put away. Books closed and on shelves, or at least in neat piles on the oak coffee table in the living room. Clothing and shoes clean, stowed in the correct drawers or closets for each child. Even the battered old desk everyone wanted to use was cleared and spotless.

Alex forced himself not to think about how long it had been since he or Etan had to pick up toys from the living room or anywhere else. He made another restless circuit of the tidy space instead.

Joining up two apartments years ago had made everything easier, more than even he expected. All their children had a room to themselves, or would later tonight.

Another thought Alex couldn't fit into his mind yet.

That empty bedroom.

He and Etan had their own space again instead of wedging a small bed into their bedroom. Whoever was starting to Dream slept in a tiny bedroom beside them now. That was about to change, too.

Their youngest showed signs of being a Witness, unerringly joining Alex either when Etan Dreamed or when one of the other children did. His long, nearly sleepless nights of sitting with several Dreamers would end long before he was ready.

After another circuit through the kitchen, brushing invisible crumbs off the tiled counter, Alex closed his eyes. He leaned back against the cool, sharp edge, tilting his head to the left, then the right.

He could walk in circles through their home for another few hours or another few days, and not a thing would change.

Caela was leaving. She was ready.

Alex had to be, too, even if he only pretended for her sake.

Leading a group up to Maple Ridge – the first group Wolf Branch had ever sent out from their own children – was a wonderful opportunity. An honor. He was thrilled for her when he stopped to consider how excited she was to be setting out on her own.

Alex didn't want her to stay forever. Not really. His mind knew it was time. That this was a good thing. He knew he and Etan and everyone else had done a wonderful job getting their community and their children to this point.

His heart was nowhere near ready, though.

He opened his eyes and walked slowly through the living room, down the hall, and through the open door of her bedroom.

Alex told himself he needed to make sure she hadn't forgotten anything. That fiction evaporated when he got a good look around.

The room might have been left empty since this building was built well over a hundred years ago. Walls stripped bare, no longer decorated with paintings by Iris, drawings by Caela. Dark hardwood floor spotless and gleaming. Drawers and closets as empty and barren as the single bed against one wall, the faded and careworn blue loveseat under a window

Alex sighed and shook his head. He'd done exactly the same when he left his parents' house at sixteen.

He hoped Caela would *want* to come home for visits, unlike his own dread of the yearly pilgrimage back to Wisconsin. He hadn't been back since he and Etan left Chicago twenty-five years ago, and only a handful of times before that.

He knew he was luckier than many parents back then, when most kids left home at eighteen, many moving away for college.

Caela seemed mostly happy to have waited until her twentieth year to strike out on her own.

She wasn't going hundreds of miles away to a big city for college like Alex had, either. Maple Ridge wasn't even twenty miles away. With no more airplanes or trains or even fast cars, that was a long journey. Still, closer than their daughter could have gone.

Alex knew he was lucky in that, too. He also knew the empty place in his heart, where Caela had been the first of their children to dwell, would feel better over time.

But it never would close up and heal all the way.

He'd done his part by getting the power set up in Maple Ridge. He'd considered trying to get himself included in the group joining them for the next few days, pretending he had more work to do. But it wasn't true.

He'd been training a bunch of modern-day engineers, eager to learn something besides farming, for a few years now. Five of them would be making this trip already. They'd all worked alongside Alex to set everything up. Each knew the systems as well as he did.

Now wasn't the time to keep pushing himself into their daughter's life.

Now was the time to trust Caela. To trust everyone with her, his own work, and everyone he'd trained.

Now was the time to stay here and let them all go.

Alex heard the apartment door open and wiped at his eyes. Whoever that was didn't need to deal with his weepy mood today.

"Dad?" Caela called.

"In here. In your room."

Thankfully their oldest smiled more than she scowled these days, and she walked in doing just that. Caela was as tall and slender as Iris, with her long curly red hair caught back in a loose ponytail. Alex knew he was miles away from impartial, but he remained convinced she grew more lovely every day.

"My *empty* room, you mean." She sat on the blue loveseat and patted the cushion beside her. "Measuring for Eddie's things?"

Alex joined her, making sure he didn't grunt. Turning fifty a couple of weeks ago didn't mean he had to sound like it. Not even on a day like this, when he felt every one of those years in his bones.

"Eddie will be in here the second you leave, measurements or not. I was just thinking."

"You've been doing a lot of that lately. All the Dreams around here should have been warning enough."

Alex laughed under his breath, then held out his arm. She leaned against him, head on his shoulder.

"Someday you'll understand. All the Dreams in the world can't prepare you for some things. Everything ready downstairs?"

"Mom Gena is in a lot worse shape than you are." Caela sat up, but she didn't shrug out from under his arm. "Mom Iris is excited about the trip, I think. Dad E seems to be holding it together so far."

"Trust me. He's just better at hiding it than I am. I expect it will hit Iris when she has to turn around and leave you up there. When are you heading out?"

"Pretty much when *you* get downstairs."

Her smile was back, big enough that Alex heard it in her voice.

"Sent to fetch the old man, huh? Another few minutes up here won't make this any easier. Another few days wouldn't."

Caela stood and held out both hands. Alex squeezed them as he got up, but he dropped them to pull her into a hug.

"I know you're ready. I'm the one who's not. I'm going to miss you, Caela."

"I'll miss you too, Dad. I'll be back more often than you think."

Alex kept his thoughts to himself as he followed her out and down the stairs.

She'd be home for a visit, sure.

Not home to stay.

Chapter 39

SEVEN GROUPS of new settlers had departed Wolf Branch since the nightmare of Mary's exile. As always, a huge crowd filled the Square, happy and excited. Several families were sending their oldest children today, so Etan suspected he wasn't the only one feeling a bit melancholy under the joy.

The biggest four-wheel-drive truck still in reliable working order was packed full of tools, supplies, and the few belongings that hadn't already made the trip up the mountain. Several smaller vehicles that could traverse the damaged road to Maple Ridge waited behind it in a line along the road.

A few parents would join the new colony for the first few days, then bring most of the vehicles back down. Iris walked along the line of supplies and milling families, pretending to inspect or organize. She knew more about Maple Ridge and the resources there than anyone else.

And if Etan didn't know better, he would have guessed she was closer to Caela's age than into her forties. Her blue jeans, t-shirt, and long black hair had her looking the same as the first day he and Alex met her and Gena. She caught Etan watching and smiled with her hand over her heart, the green fire of Anne's stone flashing in the sunlight.

Dana Chen and most of her security crew stood close to the biggest truck. Neither Etan nor anyone else on the Council liked the idea of ten guards having to go along, at least for the first few months.

No one old enough to remember the fatal nighttime raid from Maple Ridge so long ago – or Alex nearly losing his life not far from where they stood – were willing to argue. Nor was anyone who remembered the threat of Mary's broken Dreams that Caela helped them face.

A desperate, pathetic handful of those who'd followed Mary had tried to return a couple of years ago. Their ravaged skin too covered with sores to be recognizable. Not much more than bones underneath. Raving from mental and physical illness. Probably deranged from Dreams and Memories no one else wanted to know.

Too far gone to survive for more than a day or so, much less stage any kind of attack. Dana let Etan know every time it happened. Sandy assured him they met a quick and merciful end, with the method Etan remembered all too well. They all agreed it was best if no one else found out.

And best to assume it could happen again.

A hand as warm as the April sun in a cloudless blue sky found his. Etan looked down into Gena's red-rimmed eyes. His mother Laura stood behind her, close beside Iris's parents. All of them hugged Etan, their eyes showing their own pride and sadness.

Gena nodded toward the right. Alex walked down the nearly empty street, his head lowered to focus on Caela. Their daughter gestured and smiled as she spoke, no doubt describing the great adventure unfolding before her.

"He looks better than he did this morning," Gena said. "We'll have our hands full tonight."

"You'll be surprised, I think. Caela had the right idea to go get him herself instead of me."

"She's the only one of us with any sense today," his mother said.

Her real goodbyes said earlier, Caela had a quick kiss for Etan and Gena and the rest before she was off toward the center of the square. The group of seventeen heading up the mountain today all turned when she joined them.

"You two did a wonderful job raising her," Gena said, watching Caela. "They're lucky to have her as their leader."

After so many years, Etan had to admit one of the biggest advantages of a town full of Dreamers and Witnesses was no arguments over things like this. They'd all Dreamed of Caela heading up the new community in Maple Ridge. Even if she hadn't been the strongest Dreamer among them, decisions like this were incredibly easy, at least on the surface.

"She's part of *their* group now," Alex said. For the first time all day, he sounded proud instead of sad. "Head of their Council."

"Hopefully she'll go easy on us when we have to decide things together," Etan said.

The chatter all around them quieted as George Light made his slow way toward the group of new departures. His tightly curled hair was nearly all gray now, and he moved carefully after the chill of the night before. Growing fruits and berries better suited for the high altitude, and better to help with common problems like arthritis, was high on the list for the new colony.

George spoke into the hush, his voice as full and rich as ever.

"Friends and family, we're gathered for a momentous and joyful occasion. I won't lie to you after so many years, though. More than a little sadness runs through my heart today. I suspect I'm not the only one feeling that way."

George's son Daniel, a boy as strong, tall, and every bit as charismatic as his father, stood close by Caela's side. Alex took his hand, and Etan knew he'd also noticed how often the two of them ended up together.

Etan couldn't imagine a better Witness match for their daughter.

"Many of us arrived here nearly twenty-five years ago," George said. "Worried and unsure, so afraid to leave the outside world we thought was so secure behind. And terrified of leaving it too late.

"I won't tell you it's all been easy. Some of our time here has seemed nearly as dark as the old world outside. But we've made it this far together. And today, the very best of what we've accomplished stands before us, ready to set out into this new world on their own."

Etan noticed most of the Council had joined his family, standing beside and behind them. Dana Chen, her face proud and excited. Harry Mullins, not bothering to hide his tears or his smile. Most of them had children or grandchildren surrounding Caela.

"So while we're sad to see them go," George continued, "to know we won't be waking up to their voices tomorrow, to their smiles and their frowns, take comfort, my friends. These young people are the hope and promise of what brought us all together nearly a quarter of a century ago. They are the life and vitality that will see humanity through into a better future."

As the crowd shifted to let Caela and the other colonists move toward George, Etan spotted Gwen, Connor, and the rest of their children in a group of their friends. All their children were well into their teens now, smart and strong and independent. So much so that he had no idea who would want to stay in Wolf Branch and who would want to follow Caela into communities of their own making.

He hoped they would tell him and Alex before the Dreams did.

Caela stepped up beside George, and Daniel stood on his other side. George held out the traditional packet of seeds and plants despite the amounts already loaded in the trucks. Caela closed her hands over his.

"You're the first group to leave made up of our own families," George said. "You truly carry the seeds of our future. And so we offer you the gift of food so you may prosper in your new home."

"I can't add much to that," she said, grinning up at George as she held the packet to her heart. "So I'll just say thank you. To George and to all of you for coming here to see us off. Thank you to everyone who helped us get ready by going up there to get an idea of what we'd need and setting up so many things for us. Thank you to everyone who's going with us today. And thank you for being willing to leave when the time comes, even if we beg you to stay."

Behind Caela, Iris joined in the gentle laughter, but she blotted her eyes with her sleeve.

"Thank you for trusting me to do my best to keep our new

community organized. That means everything to me. I'll do my best, and I promise to ask for help *before* I need it.

"More than anything, we want to thank all of you. Our parents, our families, *all* of you. Everyone in Wolf Branch who took in a bunch of dazed settlers from the outside. Everyone who made that uncertain journey here.

"If you hadn't been so brave, so strong, none of us would be here. You left your homes, your lives, your entire world behind to give us a chance. Thank you for sharing that past world with us as much as you can. And thank you for trusting us to help you build this new one."

George raised his arms more slowly than in years past, but his gesture still managed to embrace everyone who could see him.

"Good journey!"

At the crowd's thunderous response, everyone seemed to move at once. For the first time, Etan caught a pale glimpse of what Alex saw all the time.

Patterns in the shifting crowd, the wind through the faintly budding trees around the square. Patterns in the beat of his own heart. Patterns that drove him away from here when he was younger than Caela, then brought him back home again to a life more full and joyful than he ever could have Dreamed.

Patterns that led to the man beside him, always.

Etan turned and stepped into Alex's arms.

The only home that had ever mattered.

ABOUT KARI

Kari Kilgore's wanderlust and imagination lead her all over the world on grand adventures. Her heart and family bring her home to her native Appalachian Mountains of Virginia. From that solid base, she and her husband Jason A. Adams bring those adventures to life in fiction.

Kari writes science fiction, fantasy, horror, and contemporary fiction, and she's happiest when she surprises herself. She lives at the end of a long dirt road in the middle of the woods with Jason, various house critters, and wildlife they're better off not knowing more about.

The Confidential Adventure Club

For Kari's exclusive free After The End stories and deleted scenes (including from the Storms of Future Past Series), discounts, early pre-sale releases, adorable pet photos, and a whole lot more not available anywhere else, visit The Confidential Adventure Club at www.smarturl.it/sofp-welcome.

Hope to see you there!

www.karikilgore.com
www.spiralpublishing.net

ALSO BY KARI KILGORE

I hope you enjoyed reading *Fighting the Storm* as much as I enjoyed writing it. For more of the Storms of Future Past series, swing by www.smarturl.it/storms-series. Check out more of my fiction at www.karikilgore.com.

The Confidential Adventure Club

Want to read a short story with Etan's father Connor and his grandfather Evan? Curious what happened to Etan, Alex, and Caela after The End of *Fighting the Storm*?

Want more fiction from Kari, including stories, discounts, and box sets not available anywhere else? Want to hear about locations, research, and other cool things that inspired this story and beyond? All that and adorable pet photos, too?

Join The Confidential Adventure Club for an exclusive thank you gift of an After the End story from *Fighting the Storm* and a whole lot more at www.smarturl.it/sofp-welcome.

Hope to see you there!

Novels:

Until Death

The Dream Thief

Dreaming the Storm: Book One of the Storms of Future Past Series

Joining the Storm: Book Two of the Storms of Future Past Series

Novellas:

Songs in the Mountain

Legacy of the Land

Restricted Species

The Becalmed

In the Pines

Into the Storm: Book Three of the Storms of Future Past Series

Short Stories:

Renovations

Intentions

The Garbage Belt

The Seeds of Love

Wicked Bone

The Sound of Murder

Terminalia

Little Five: A Terminalia Story

Reflections

Collections:

Fantastic Women: A Dark Fantasy Novella Trio

Fantastic Shorts: Volume 1 - A Fantasy Short Story Collection

"Kari Kilgore is an author to watch—her lyrical voice a siren song; her insight, conjured voodoo."

—Richard Thomas, author of *Breaker* and *Tribulations*